"Chase You?" He Couldn't Be Serious!

A low burn sparked to life deep inside her. Talk about ego! He might be God's gift to every other single woman in the state, but all she wanted from him was his support for the funding bill.

Suddenly, mischief sparkled in her eyes. Denying it would do no good. A half smile flirted with her mouth. "There seems to be a misunderstanding here," she said softly.

With painstaking slowness, she trailed her finger up his tie, to the collar of his shirt, to the skin just below his ear. Lifting her hand to his mouth, she dared to trace the full, sensuous line of his lower lip. "If I were chasing you, I wouldn't hesitate to do this. But just for the record, that's not what I'm doing. I'm walking away."

Philly dropped her hand and summoned every ounce of control she possessed. "Good night, Congressman. Pleasant dreams."

Dear Reader:

What makes a Silhouette Desire hero? This is a question I often ask myself—it's part of my job to think about these things!—and I *know* it's something you all think about, too. I like my heroes rugged, sexy and sometimes a little infuriating. I love the way our heroes are sometimes just a little bit in the dark about love . . . *and* about what makes the heroine "tick." It's all part of their irresistible charm.

This March, I want you all to take a good look at our heroes and—if you want—let me know what you think about them!

Naturally, we have a *Man of the Month* who just can't be beat—Dane Lassiter in Diana Palmer's *The Case of the Mesmerizing Boss.* This story is doubly good because not only is it a *Man of the Month* title, it's also the first book in Diana Palmer's new *series,* called MOST WANTED. As for Lassiter, he's a hero you're not likely to ever forget.

Do you think playboys can be tamed? I certainly do! And you can watch one really get his comeuppance in Linda Turner's delightful *Philly and the Playboy.* Barbara McCauley creates a sexy, mountain man (is there any other kind?) in *Man From Cougar Pass,* and Carole Buck brings us a hero who's a bit more citified—but no less intriguing—in *Knight and Day.* And if a seafaring fellow is the type for you, don't miss Donna Carlisle's *Cast Adrift.*

Some heroes—like some real-life men—are less than perfect, and I have to admit I had a few doubts about Lass Small's *Dominic.* But so many of you wrote in asking for his story that I began to wonder if Dominic shouldn't have equal time to state his case. (You'll remember he gave Tate Lambert such a hard time in *Goldilocks and the Behr.*) Is Dominic a hero? I think he very well might be, but I'm interested in hearing what you all thought about this newly tamed man.

So, I've said all I have to say *except* that I do wish you best wishes for happy reading. Now I'm waiting to hear from you.

Until next month,

Lucia Macro
Senior Editor

LINDA TURNER

PHILLY AND THE PLAYBOY

SILHOUETTE *Desire*

Published by Silhouette Books New York

America's Publisher of Contemporary Romance

SILHOUETTE BOOKS
300 East 42nd St., New York, N.Y. 10017

PHILLY AND THE PLAYBOY

ISBN: 0-373-05701-6

First Silhouette Books printing March 1992

All the characters in this book have no existence outside the imagination of the author and have no relation whatsoever to anyone bearing the same name or names. They are not even distantly inspired by any individual known or unknown to the author, and all incidents are pure invention.

Printed in the U.S.A.

Books by Linda Turner

Silhouette Desire

A Glimpse of Heaven #220
Wild Texas Rose #653
Philly and the Playboy #701

Silhouette Intimate Moments

The Echo of Thunder #238
Crosscurrents #263
An Unsuspecting Heart #298
Flirting with Danger #316
Moonlight and Lace #354

Silhouette Special Edition

Shadows in the Night #350

LINDA TURNER

began reading romances in high school and began
writing them one night when she had nothing else to
read. She's been writing ever since. Single and living
in Texas, she travels every chance she gets, scouting
locales for her books.

One

The press conference wouldn't begin for another fifteen minutes, but the reporters were already starting to gather in the cafeteria of Bethesda's Franklin Shelter for the Homeless like buzzards circling a road kill. Anticipation built as smoke lazily spiraled toward the ceiling from the numerous cigarettes lit with total disregard for the No Smoking signs placed at regular intervals around the room. The local print media had the place covered like a blanket, but a gratifying number of television reporters had shown up, as well. At the back of the room the crew from the ABC affiliate was setting up for a live remote for their noon show.

Philadelphia O'Neil watched the procedure from the open doorway of the shelter's office and swallowed a ragged laugh that was nothing but nerves and pure daring. Dear God, could she do this? she wondered wildly. Could she really carry this off? When she'd accepted the position of director of the shelter a month ago, she'd known that dealing with the press was going to be one of her least favorite parts of the job. She wasn't an extrovert looking for her share of the limelight; she was at her best when she dealt with people one on one. But her back was against the wall, and she was desperate. Before lunch was over, most of Maryland and no doubt all of Capitol Hill would once again be talking about her and Congressman Morgan Stewart II.

At her side, Gary Kramer, her assistant, silently took in the size of the crowd before turning back to her, his brown eyes alight with amused suspicion. "Okay, how'd you manage it? You didn't get twenty reporters down here by telling them you were going to discuss the Appropriation Committee's upcoming vote on the new shelter funding bill. What'd you do? Promise them a sex scandal, or what?"

The dimples framing her mouth flashed with a mixture of guilt and mischief, giving her fine-boned, delicate face a decidedly spritely appearance. "Not exactly," she hedged. "I simply mentioned that I would have something of interest to say about our playboy congressman."

Gary couldn't help but grin. There were several bachelor congressmen, but only one Philly spoke of in just that way. Grandson of a late Speaker of the House and the last of a long line of distinguished politicians, Maryland's Morgan Stewart II was the product of exceptional breeding, old money and class. He garnered votes and women with a charm that was legendary, but there was more to the man than just his famous smile. Already a force to be reckoned with in the House after just two terms, he could be as persuasive as the Devil sweet-talking a sinner when he needed support for one of his pet projects. But he could also be as immovable as Mt. Rushmore when he was opposed to a bill. He'd made no secret of the fact that he was dead set against increased funding for the homeless. And as a key member of the Appropriation Committee, there was a good possibility he had the votes to kill the bill before it ever made it to the House floor for debate.

The very idea of anyone having that much power outraged Philadelphia. The very day she had become the shelter's new director, she had started a letter-writing campaign against the congressman and flooded his office with mail. Determined to change his mind, she then followed up with a barrage of phone calls that never got past his watchdog of a secretary. Frustrated but undaunted, she took the protest to the public by firing off a sizzling letter to the editor of the *Washington Post,* who'd promptly printed it. An hour after it hit the streets, Stewart called *her,* demanding to know what the devil she thought she was doing. The war had begun.

That had been four weeks ago, and since then they'd argued on the phone a half-dozen times and, to the delight of Washington readers, continued to trade quips in the *Post.* Neither side had budged an inch, and the battle of wills showed no sign of abating. Time, however, was on Stewart's side. If he could stall a vote on the funding bill until Congress's fall recess, it would never make it out of committee.

Studying the glint in Philly's green eyes, Gary had a sinking feeling she'd finally decided to pull out all the stops. "Whatever it is, he's not going to like it, is he?"

Laughing, her shrug was sassy. "Relax," she retorted with a grin that did nothing to dispel his uneasiness. "I know what I'm doing. So far, Stewart's been able to hold his own in the papers. But how good is he at handling a public challenge?"

The laughter fell from Gary's round face as if she'd slapped him. "You can't be serious! This is Morgan Stewart we're talking about, not some wet-behind-the-ears freshman congressman out to make a name for himself. He may have been born with a silver spoon in his mouth, but he hasn't gotten where he has in Congress by wimping out. He knows how to fight. And how to win. You drop this on him without warning, and all you're going to do is antagonize him."

She wanted to cry that the people who found themselves out on the street after years of hard work didn't get any warning, so why should Stewart? But she knew Gary was right. She didn't want the congressman as an enemy, she just wanted him to listen to her. He had to. Without his support, the funding bill was dead in the water. Politicians! she thought in disgust. All they were good for was dragging their feet and creating more red tape. Whoever invented them should have been shot.

Her jaw set at a determined angle, she abruptly turned back into her office and reached for the phone

on her desk. "All right, then I'll give him a warning," she said as she punched out his number from
memory. "He'll need time to prepare a statement."

"I guess I should have expected this. After all, I
watched it happen to all my friends. A woman grows
old and feeble and her family just doesn't want to be
bothered with her anyone. Everyone has their own
lives, their own problems, and they don't have time to
be concerned about grandma rumbling around in a
great big house all by herself." A heavy sigh traveled
easily across the phone line. "Oh, well, don't worry
about me. I'll get by somehow. I always do."

Morgan leaned back in his leather office chair and
propped his feet up on his desk. Beneath his dark
brown mustache, a wide grin split his finely chiseled
face. His grandmother didn't fool him in the least with
her sob story. At seventy-eight, Augusta Stewart had
more energy and zest for life than a person half her
age. She was on the board of directors of more charities than he could keep up with and still managed to
handle the considerable estate his grandfather had left
her like a master accountant. And she detested anyone calling her grandma.

But she did have a legitimate beef. He tried to talk
to her on the phone at least once a week, but it had
been months since he'd been able to actually stop by
and see her. Every time he made plans to do just that,
something came up. Besides his usual congressional
work schedule, he was up to his neck in a reelection
campaign that had turned dirty, thanks to his opponent, Hollis King. The man was a snake in the grass

who wouldn't know a scruple if he tripped over it, but he was smart enough to show the voters nothing but charm. Morgan hadn't been able to relax his guard so much as a minute without losing points in the polls.

"So you're all alone now, are you?" he teased, his blue eyes sparkling with devilment. "Then I guess Lillie must have quit her job as housekeeper. No wonder you're upset. She's been with you since the beginning of time."

"No, of course Lillie hasn't—"

"And then there's your new tenant in the apartment over the garage," he cut in, playfully needling her. "You did tell me you'd found someone, didn't you? What happened? She skip town when this month's rent came due?"

"Of course not," she huffed. "She would never leave me in the lurch that way." Only someone who knew Augusta Stewart very well would have noticed the subtle shift in her suddenly too innocent tone. "She's a wonderful girl. Why don't you stop by tonight and meet her?"

Morgan smothered a laugh. When Gussy first told him of her new renter weeks ago, she'd described the woman as something of an eccentric who had never married, no doubt because she never did the expected. Now she was a wonderful "girl." Morgan could almost hear the matchmaking wheels turning in Gussy's head.

"Nice try, Gus, but your delivery needs a little work. Next time try for a little less innocence."

"Why, I don't know what you're talking about," she gasped indignantly.

Morgan might have been fooled if he hadn't gotten the distinct impression she was trying hard not to laugh. Enjoying himself, he arched a mocking brow. "No? I would have sworn you were trying to set me up."

"And what's wrong with that?" she sniffed. "I've been keeping track of the campaign. I know how hard you're working. An evening with a decent woman would be good for you."

"The last time I needed your help getting a date, I was twelve years old," he reminded her dryly. "Back off, sweetheart—"

Tim Maxwell, his campaign manager and right-hand man, suddenly knocked at his office door and stepped inside, his square face grim. "Sorry to interrupt, but you've got another call on line two."

During the course of the campaign, Morgan had seen that look on Tim's face often enough to know it could mean only one thing. Trouble. He swung his feet to the floor. "Who is it?"

"Philadelphia O'Neil."

Morgan swore under his breath and turned his attention back to his grandmother. "Sorry, Gussy. Something's come up. Gotta go. I'll try to call you back later."

Hanging up, he scowled at the blinking light on the phone, his eyes glinting with the light of battle. He was, he reminded himself, an open-minded man. He didn't expect all his constituents to agree with his position on any particular issue, and he welcomed their comments. But from the day he'd received her first letter, Philadelphia O'Neil had damn near flooded him out of his office with her "comments." Then she'd started calling, demanding to speak to him personally.

Irritated by her tactics and what he knew was unjustified criticism, he'd been anxious to take her calls and defend himself. But Tim had stopped him, advising him to limit his response to letters because an ill-advised word spoken in haste to the wrong person could be political suicide during an election year.

It should have ended there, but the damn woman had refused to accept his silence. She'd started taking potshots at him in the paper, taking a perverse pleasure in seeing just how far she could push him. He had responded in kind and let the matter ride. But when she persisted and portrayed him as a cold, unfeeling Scrooge who couldn't be bothered with anyone whose income wasn't at least six figures, he had hit the roof. She knew nothing about him. Nothing! Although he didn't advertise it, he made a sizable donation to a number of charities each year, and the last three major public assistance bills would have never made it through the House without his strong backing. Ignoring Tim's warnings, he'd called her.

During that first conversation and every one that had followed, he'd tried reasoning with her, charming her and flat out arguing with her. Yet for every point he'd scored off her, she had scored another, annoying the hell out of him. If he hadn't known better, he would have sworn she was a politician. But he couldn't deny he looked forward to pitting himself against her sharp wit and even sharper tongue.

Leaning back in his chair, he punched line two, a wolfish smile of anticipation flirting with the corners of his mouth. "Ms. O'Neil," he said smoothly. "Is this a social call, or should I put on my battle gear?"

The quick quip Philly had planned to greet him with was nearly forgotten in the sudden need to smile. Drat the man, she would not let him disarm her so easily! "Actually, it's a temporary cease-fire," she said with a coolness that didn't even hint at the nervousness churning in her stomach. "I think it's time we tried to work out a truce."

Through the sudden silence that throbbed on the line, she could almost feel his surprise. "Would you care to repeat that?" he replied with an innocence that made her dimples flash in appreciation. "There must be something wrong with this phone. I could have sworn you said something about a truce."

"I wouldn't start to gloat just yet if I were you, Congressman. You haven't heard my terms."

"Which are?"

"Watch Channel Three's news show today at noon. You'll find out everything you need to know then."

He frowned. She was up to something; he could feel it in his bones. "Why don't you just tell me now?"

"Can't. Haven't got time. I just wanted to give you fair warning."

He stiffened. "Fair warning? Damn it, O'Neil, what are you up to?"

"Watch the news and find out." Before he could say another word, she quietly hung up.

"Hell!" Slamming the phone back into its cradle, Morgan's eyes shot to the clock on the wall. Twelve-o-one. Swearing softly, he snatched up the remote control to the television in the corner and pressed the power switch.

"What's she done now?" Tim asked in alarm.

"Only God knows. She warned me to watch the noon news on channel Three." Glaring at the TV screen as it gradually lightened, he said, "The woman's nothing but trouble! A bleeding heart liberal with a cause. I bet she doesn't even have a life away from her work. How could she? She's too busy making mine miserable—"

On the television the picture focused on the noon anchor, then cut away to a Minicam shot of a diminutive woman nearly dwarfed by a stand of microphones. Stunned, Morgan almost choked on the hot words of exasperation that lodged in his throat. This couldn't be the same stubborn, persistent Philadelphia O'Neil who had spent the better part of a month driving him crazy. She was too young—she couldn't be twenty-four if she was a day—too small and delicate, with a disconcerting air of innocence that a woman with her looks had no business having. Dressed in a long, flowing rose skirt and frilly white blouse, her black hair tumbling in wild curls halfway down her back, she looked nothing like the sharp-tongued, aggressive woman he'd pictured in his mind every time she'd infuriated him.

Before he could stop himself, Morgan ran his gaze over the creamy skin of her oval face, the dimpled cheeks pink with nervousness, the large green eyes that seemed to twinkle with a secret, the soft, crushable mouth. Distracted, his eyes locked on the unconsciously sensuous movement of her reddened lips. It was several long moments before the statement she was making filtered through his fogged brain. He stiffened.

"...all know about my friendly disagreement with Congressman Stewart." At the muffled laughter that spread through the reporters, her dimples flashed. "Okay, so we've taken a few potshots at each other. If I got a little hostile at times, it's only because the shelter funding bill is so important." Taking a steadying breath, she looked squarely into the camera from Channel Three. "I know the congressman isn't an insensitive man. The only reason I can think of for his refusal to support the bill is that he obviously doesn't understand the heartache of homelessness. So I'm challenging him to work here at the shelter for five nights, to talk to the homeless, to meet them face-to-face and see their needs. If he can do that and still vote against the increase, then he's not the man I thought he was. Now if there are any questions..."

Realizing the implications of such a challenge, the reporters surged forward, throwing questions at her, demanding to know how well she knew the congressman, whom she supported in the upcoming election. But the local station switched back to the noon anchor before she answered a single question. "At five, we hope to bring you Congressman Stewart's response to this unexpected challenge, as well as Hollis King's reaction. As you know, King has narrowed the gap in his race for Stewart's House seat by stressing the difference between his middle class background and Stewart's wealthy one and claiming he is more sympathetic to the plight of the average citizen. If Congressman Stewart declines today's challenge, it could be a serious setback for—''

Cursing, Morgan hit the power switch. In the outer office a phone rang. It was only a single call, but he'd been in politics long enough to know it was just the first of many. His mouth compressed into a hard, thin line of fury. His little nemesis had conveniently left out his side of the issue and said just enough to make him sound like an uncaring monster.

Echoing his thoughts, Tim said flatly, "She has to be working for King. It'd be just like him to set you up like this. Whatever you do, you lose. You stick to your guns and vote down the bill, you're an unfeeling bastard. Vote for it, and you're just trying to win votes." He swore and began to pace, patting his pockets for the cigarettes he'd sworn off months ago. "Damn, I need a cigarette!"

Morgan tossed him a pack of gum, his expression harsh. "You know, there's another possibility here we haven't considered. She could just be after me."

If any other man had suggested such a thing, he would have sounded like an egotistical jackass who believed he was God's gift to womankind. But Tim had gone through school with Morgan. From the time they were fourteen years old, he'd watched girls and women chase his friend to the point of making fools of themselves. With his usual good manners Morgan had handled them all with charm, enjoying the attention as any man would. Until one had made the mistake of teaching him that it was more than his good looks she was after. The Stewart name and money were a hell of an attraction in their own right. That was when he'd learned to be leery of any woman who deliberately placed herself in his path.

Philadelphia O'Neil *had* popped into his life like a weed popping up in a garden overnight. Stopping his pacing long enough to consider the possibility, Tim finally shook his head. "Maybe, but I don't think so. This has King written all over it. Think about it," he urged. "You know how important timing is in a campaign. A month ago King's popularity was in the cellar. He had to know he needed a miracle to turn things around. Enter Philadelphia O'Neil. The very day she starts protesting your stand on the funding bill, he starts hammering at your family wealth as if it were a character flaw. Suddenly your record doesn't count for squat and the main issue of the campaign is rich versus poor."

And in a year when the economy was slumping and money was tight, Morgan knew King's message was a powerful lure for people who were dissatisfied with their lives. They only heard what they wanted to hear, and right now they were listening to King. And Philadelphia O'Neil.

"What do we have on her?"

"The return address she put on all her letters was for the shelter, but she's not living there. So I put Robertson on the case. If she's got any secrets, Robertson will ferret them out. He promised he'd have something by this afternoon."

Reaching across his desk, Morgan buzzed for his secretary. Within thirty seconds flat, Mary Barker appeared in the doorway. A short, birdlike woman with iron gray hair and perceptive brown eyes, she had been Morgan's secretary for as long as he'd held office, and his grandfather's before that. She never failed to speak her mind.

"I hope you plan to schedule a response to that O'Neil woman's press conference," she said heatedly before he could even open his mouth. "The phones are ringing off the hook!"

Morgan grinned. "Set up a press conference for five o'clock. And see if you can get all the Maryland stations to pick it up. I'm going to give Miss O'Neil a taste of her own medicine."

With his jaw set and his eyes hard, he was the spitting image of his grandfather, who had never backed down from a fight in his life. Making a quick note on her steno pad, Mary glanced up. "Anything else?"

"Has Robertson's report come in yet?"

"Not yet. I'll bring it in as soon as it arrives."

He nodded. "Instruct the staff to tell the callers that my position hasn't changed. To get people off the streets, we've got to put them back to work. And the only way to do that is with job training programs."

"I'll get right on it," Mary promised, and hurried out.

In the silence that followed her leave-taking, he said quietly, "Since I'm damned regardless of what I do, I'm going with gut instinct. I'm accepting the challenge."

To do anything else would have been political suicide. His mind already working on what the loss of five evenings during the last month before the election could do to the campaign, Tim moved to the computer and information center set up against one wall. "This is going to shoot your schedule straight to hell, but there's not a damn thing we can do about it. If we can't get somebody to stand in for you, we're going to have to cancel some appearances. How about your grandmother? Think she'd do it?"

A grin curled up one corner of Morgan's mouth. "I don't know. I'll ask her. During her younger days, she was hell on wheels on the campaign trail. My grandfather used to say he couldn't have gotten elected dogcatcher without her."

"Then maybe we should get her to respond to Miss O'Neil's challenge," Tim said, chuckling. "She could put her in her place without breaking a sweat."

Morgan's smile tightened with cynicism, his blue eyes darkening with the promise of revenge. "She'll have to get in line. Philadelphia O'Neil is mine. By the time I'm finished, she's going to regret the day she ever decided to take me on."

He would have enjoyed relishing that idea for a moment or two, but he didn't have the time. He was speaking at the Chesapeake Women's Society tonight, and the speech he had planned would now need to be completely reworked. "I'm tossing out tonight's speech," he announced, "and hitting them with the homeless."

Lifting the phone, he rang the office of one of his four legislative assistants and requested statistics on the homeless, everything from the number of shelters today compared to three years ago to the length of stay and the number of people who eventually found work and those that just moved on to the next shelter. He wanted enough ammunition to blow Philadelphia O'Neil and Hollis King right out of the water!

When Mary Barker stepped into the office an hour later with Robertson's report, Morgan and Tim were still hammering out the new speech. It was a delicate process. Statistics proved that money was definitely needed for job training, but you couldn't ignore the fact that most cities were woefully unprepared for the number of people already on the streets. And if the economy worsened, those numbers would go through the roof.

But at the sight of the large yellow envelope in Mary's hand, all work stopped. Morgan gave her a sharp look. "Is that Robertson's report?"

She nodded. "It just came in." A puzzled frown knitted her brow. "He suggested you sit down before you read it, but when I asked him why, he just said you'd find out soon enough."

"So she is working for King," Tim said in satisfaction as Morgan took the envelope and perched on the side of his desk to open it. "I knew it! His fingerprints are all over it. I wonder how much he's paying her."

"Whatever it is, it won't be enough when I expose her to the press," Morgan promised. Drawing out the report that gave the intimate details of Philadelphia O'Neil's life, he frowned at his suddenly irritating reluctance to read it. What the hell was wrong with him? he thought in growing annoyance. The woman had made herself his enemy the minute she'd stepped in front of the press and implied that he wasn't concerned with the less fortunate. He had a right to know who and what she was.

Determinedly he scanned the top sheet, but he got no further than the middle of the page before he stopped in surprise. "Oh, God, she's a flower child!"

Tim looked at him as if he had lost his mind. "What are you talking about? She couldn't have been more than a baby in the sixties."

"A baby in a hippie commune," Morgan replied. "Her parents were hippies."

"So?"

"So I'm not talking about draft dodgers and pot smokers who sat around listening to sitar music all day. When they talked about peace and love, they really meant it." He flipped to the next page, shaking his head in wonder. "Using a commune in Virginia as home base, they've spent the last twenty-five years working with Vista and the Peace Corps, the American Indian, the poor in the Appalachians and just about every other underprivileged group you can think of. And everywhere they went, they took Philadelphia right along with them."

Cynical to the end, Tim only shrugged. "She wouldn't be the first do-gooder to rebel against self-sacrifice and turn mercenary. When did she first get hooked up with King?"

Morgan turned to the third page, then the fourth, noting friends, schools, the men in her life. Was she sleeping with King? The thought hit him from out of the blue, infuriating him. What the hell difference did it make to him? He swore under his breath, not sure if he was relieved or angered that there was no mention of Hollis King anywhere. "If there's a connection between them, Robertson didn't find it."

"What about her employment record?" the other man suggested. "At one time or another she must have worked with one of King's sleazy cronies."

Her job history was on the last page. Morgan shook his head at the length of it. "She's been working since she was sixteen. Nursing homes, orphanages, Meals on Wheels during college. Then social work at different shelters. She's made something of a name for herself as a fund-raiser, which is one of the reasons the board of directors of the Franklin Shelter went out on a limb and hired her in spite of her age."

"Then there must be a connection somewhere else. For all we know, she could be the old fogey's mistress. Who's paying her rent? Where's she living?"

Morgan's eyes dropped to the bottom of the page in search of her current address. At his sharply indrawn breath Tim's stomach clenched with dread. "What is it? What's wrong?"

Feeling like he'd been kicked in the gut, Morgan lifted blue eyes that were dark with growing fury. "She lives in the apartment over my grandmother's garage. She's her new renter!"

Two

The first cold snap of the season whistled through the city's darkening streets, scattering pedestrians like autumn leaves as they hurried to escape the icy touch of the wind. Tires screeched and horns honked as rush hour traffic backed up. The shelter, usually only half-filled at this hour, was already near capacity. From the cafeteria the din of clattering dishes and flatware was accompanied by the thin wail of a baby who refused to be comforted. In the lounge a handful of children who had already eaten played chase, ignoring their mothers' commands to be quiet. No one but Philly seemed to notice the importance of the news being broadcast on the TV in the corner.

Filling the screen, Morgan Stewart stood on the steps of the Capitol and faced a crowd of reporters with the ease of a man who had been born to spend his life in the public eye. He was impeccably dressed in a charcoal silk suit, his long, lean body relaxed, his famous smile sure and confident as he expertly fielded the questions fired at him. At first glance he fairly oozed charm and affability, but Philly knew the eyes of a street fighter when she saw one. Dark with emotion, they spoke volumes as he confirmed he had every intention of accepting her challenge.

"Actually, I think it's an excellent idea," he conceded graciously, casually slipping one hand into the pocket of his slacks. "It will give me a chance to show Ms. O'Neil that I'm not the ogre she thinks I am."

"You and Ms. O'Neil have waged quite a war in the last few weeks, Congressman," a voice called out above the chuckles that followed his statement. "After everything that's been said, do you think you two will be able to work together?"

He shrugged. "Only time will tell, but I don't see why we can't. We're both reasonable adults. We're both concerned about the homeless. We just have different ways of solving the problem. Working together for a week will give me time to convince Ms. O'Neil that this is a complex issue that can't be solved simply by building bigger and better shelters."

"So you're planning to change her mind rather than change yours," a reporter called out.

It was a statement rather than a question. Morgan didn't even attempt to deny it. "I've done extensive research on this issue. I doubt that Ms. O'Neil can show me anything that would lead me to alter my current position."

Philly never heard the network reporter give a summary of Morgan's statement, then cut back to the local station. So he thought he could change her mind, did he? she mused, her green eyes glinting dangerously. With nothing more than a snap of his fingers, a flash of his devilish smile and a wink, he expected her to abandon the convictions of a lifetime. Not bloody well likely! He might be able to charm votes out of every female voter under the age of a hundred and two, but he would soon discover that he wasn't dealing with some vain, eyelash-fluttering, empty-headed bimbo. She wasn't her parents' daughter for nothing. She knew how to stand her guard, fight for a cause— *But she wasn't supposed to be fighting with him.*

The thought brought her up short. Too late, she remembered the whole point of her challenge was to try to reach him, to get past the public figure to the usually inaccessible and private, caring man underneath. The man Gussy had assured her was there, the man Gussy had urged her to challenge. The man Philly knew now she was going to find it next to impossible to work with.

Dear God, why had she ever let Gussy talk her into this?

"Philly?"

Startled at the sight of the masculine fingers suddenly wriggling in front of her nose, she glanced up to find Gary standing in front of her, a frown of concern etching his brow. "What's wrong?"

"Silk Sally just took the last bed, and she's insisting that flea-bitten hound of hers be allowed to sleep

with her." Expecting her to smile at the mention of the
fiercely independent bag lady who had earned her
nickname by carrying all of her possessions in a tat-
tered silk pillowcase, his eyes narrowed. "You want to
tell me what's going on? I heard the news about Stewart. I thought you'd be thrilled."

She snorted at that. "Thrilled? Didn't you hear
what he said? He's going to try to change *my* mind!
He's already made up his."

"Are you afraid he can?"

"Of course not! But working with him's not going
to be easy."

He lifted a brow in surprise. "Did you expect it to
be?"

"No."

"Then what's bothering you? Don't you think you
can handle the playboy congressman?"

Her chin went up at that. "You know better than
that. I can take anything Morgan Stewart dishes out."

He grinned. "I know that. I just wanted to make
sure you did. Now will you please go talk to Silk Sally?
Every time I try to tell her pets aren't allowed inside,
she turns off her damn hearing aid!"

After that, Philly hardly had time to sit down, let
alone worry about Morgan Stewart. Convincing Sally
to leave her dog outside in the storeroom was the least
of her problems. As the hour grew later and the temperature colder, stragglers wandered in off the street
looking for beds that just weren't available. If it had
been left up to her, Philly would have made them all
pallets on the floor, but there were legal limits on how

many people she could let in the door. Cursing bu-
reaucrats who had no idea what it was like to turn
someone back out into the cold night, she got on the
phone and called all the shelters in the D.C. area until
she found a bed for every latecomer. No one would
sleep outside if she had anything to say about it!

By nine-thirty, every shelter within a fifty-mile ra-
dius was full, and she was exhausted. Families were
settling down for the night and Philly thought long-
ingly of home and her own bed. Finishing up the last
of her paperwork, she locked up her desk and reached
for her coat. Suddenly a dog barked sharply near the
shelter's front entrance. She groaned. She should have
known she couldn't trust Silk Sally to leave Jethro in
the storeroom. Muttering under her breath, she
quickly shrugged into her coat and grabbed her purse
before hurrying out of her office.

But when she reached the sign-in desk, Silk Sally
and her dog were nowhere in sight. Instead a weary
couple and their three small sons surrounded a helpless Gary, pleading with him to find a place for them.
He tried to explain that the shelter was already full to
the rafters, but the excited barking of the family's
black Labrador retriever nearly drowned him out.

"Thank God!" he sighed in relief when he saw
Philly rushing toward them. "I tried to make them
understand that the fire marshal limits the number of
people we can take in—"

"But we have nowhere else to go," the mother cut
in quietly, her thin shoulders weighted with despair.
"We just got into town today—my husband's looking for work. And it's so cold out. The children . . ."

"They get sick so easy," the father said gruffly. "If you'll just let us stay here tonight, I'll pay you for the lodgings just as soon as I get a job."

Philly had heard that same humble promise more times than she cared to remember, but it still broke her heart. No one should have to plead for shelter in the night for their children. She stepped forward. "No payment is necessary, Mister—"

"Cartwright," he supplied hesitantly. "Joseph Cartwright, ma'am. This is my wife, Molly, and my boys... Mike, Stephen and Joey." Shushing the dog, he added, "And this is Blacky."

Acknowledging the introductions with a nod and a smile, she turned her attention back to the rail-thin man who stood straight and tall before her, clinging to his dignity even under the most trying of circumstances. She ached to assure him that she understood his plight, but sometimes it took nothing more than a hint of commiseration, a trace of sympathy, to break a proud man. She held out her hand to him and introduced herself, explaining regretfully, "I'm afraid what Gary told you is true. We have a limited number of beds and they were filled hours ago. I'd offer to try to get you into one of the other shelters, but I know for a fact that they're full, as well. I'm sorry."

The small spark of hope that had burned in the depths of his eyes flickered and died. He sighed tiredly and turned back toward the entrance. "We appreciate the thought, anyway, ma'am. Don't worry about us. We'll find something. We have to."

Philly knew she had no reason to feel guilty. She had a clear-cut set of rules to follow under such circumstances, procedures that tied her hands as effectively as handcuffs. But how could anyone with any heart at all expect her to stand there and watch those defeated parents lead their three boys back out into the bitterly cold night?

"Wait!"

"Philly—"

She heard the warning note in Gary's voice, but it was too late. Hang the rules! She knew it wasn't wise to get personally involved, but she'd been lost the minute she'd looked into Molly Cartwright's tired brown eyes and seen nothing but defeat. "You can come home with me for the night," she said in a voice that would brook no argument. "You and your wife can have the spare room and the kids can take the hide-a-bed. My car's parked in the back. Let's go."

Gussy's large Tudor home was located in the middle of a quiet neighborhood of aged but elegant mansions, pristine lawns, ancient magnolias and understated class. Considering her wealth and background and the powerful position her late husband had held in Congress for so many years, Gussy, like many of her neighbors, should have been a snob. But Philly knew she wouldn't blink an eye at the thought of penniless strangers sleeping in the apartment over her garage. Not only was the older woman on the board of directors of the shelter, she volunteered there as often as her busy schedule permitted. If she'd been working there tonight, she'd have invited the Cartwrights home with her without a moment's hesitation.

"Do you live *here?*"

"Geez, it looks like a place where a princess lives, doesn't it, Mom? It's so big!"

Philly smiled at the awed exclamations of the boys. She'd been just as stunned the first time she'd seen the house. She'd nearly been homeless herself, everything she owned having been lost in a fire the week after she became director of the shelter. When Gussy had offered her the apartment over her garage at a ridiculously low rent, Philly had taken it without even checking the place out. The day she'd arrived to move in and realized she was going to live on one of the finest estates in Maryland, she had been shocked speechless.

"Actually, I live here," she said, driving past the house to the back and bringing her VW Bug to a stop in front of the three-car garage that was a scaled-down replica of the house, complete with stained-glass windows. "It's a lot smaller than the big house, but sometimes it does make me feel like a princess. Come on in."

Crammed into the small car, the kids waited until their parents climbed out before tumbling out with a whoop of glee, anxious to explore. Blacky, catching their excitement, scrambled after them just as Gussy switched on the back light and opened the back door. "Philly? Is that you? I thought I heard children—"

She never had a chance to finish her sentence. Blacky spied Gussy's huge black and white tomcat, Mighty Mouse, at her feet and barked in delight. Tongue lolling, eyes dancing, he made a beeline straight for the cat.

"Oh, no!"

"Blacky, stop!"

"Watch it, Gussy—"

Gussy jumped out of the way with surprising alacrity, her nightgown and robe hiked up to her knees. "My lord, where did that monster come from?" she exclaimed. "Get him, Mighty Mouse!"

But the cat took one good look at the dog that outweighed him by a good sixty pounds and decided to make a hasty retreat. With a yowl of protest, he turned tail and shot back into the house. A heartbeat later Blacky streaked through the still-open door like a dark bullet, with the children hard on his heels. The chase was on.

Philly tried not to laugh, she really did. But no one enjoyed sheer, unadulterated pandemonium more than she did. The animals were racing through the house as if it were an obstacle course, while the yelling kids struggled to keep up. The Cartwrights, obviously afraid they would be thrown off the property as soon as order was restored, raced after their wayward sons and outlaw dog, rescuing vases and furniture and demanding at the top of their lungs that they all behave *this* instant! Gussy, not even lifting an eyebrow at the reality of having her house taken over by strangers, merely straightened her nightclothes and said with some surprise, "Well, this certainly shoots Mighty Mouse's tough cat image all to hell, doesn't it?"

It was too much. Letting out a peal of laughter, Philly wiped at the tears that gathered in her eyes.

"Poor baby. Once word of this gets out, he'll be the laughingstock of the neighborhood."

"There'll be no living with him," Gussy said in disgust as she stepped inside. "You know how arrogant he is when he gets his nose out of joint."

Suddenly, from upstairs, Blacky bayed like a hound who'd finally cornered a wily fox. Philly grinned. "I guess I'd better go rescue him before he's completely embarrassed."

She headed for the stairs in the foyer, only to find the whole menagerie clattering down the steps at a dead run, with Mighty Mouse in the lead. She didn't even glance at the cat as he whizzed past her but instead moved to block the pursuing dog's path, bracing herself like a linebacker preparing for a game-winning tackle. Undaunted, Blacky headed straight for her.

Arms spread to catch him, she told herself he would stop. But he never even checked his speed. Sporting what looked suspiciously like a wicked canine grin at the new game she'd started, he flew right into her arms.

Philly never heard the front door open behind her. Knocked on her backside by the force of the impact, she tightened her grip on the squirming Labrador and laughingly evaded his licking tongue. Turning her head aside, she cried, "Oh, yuck! Stop, you beast—"

Whatever else she was going to say died at the sight of the man towering over her, his feet only inches from her posterior on the marble tiled floor, his razor-sharp blue eyes boring into hers, snatching her breath before she'd even thought to note the danger. Dazed, she couldn't drag her gaze from his, her one inane thought that now she knew why women had been known to drop their teeth at the sight of Morgan Stewart II. And it had nothing to do with his looks.

Oh, he was handsome—she'd give him that. His shock of thick dark brown hair, the refined lines of his sculptured face and the athletic grace of his long, lean body were certainly easy on the eye. But there was a suppressed power about him, a mischievousness hinted at in the dimples that framed his mouth, a passion that seemed to smolder in the depths of his dark blue eyes that any woman with any blood in her veins would find next to impossible to resist.

And she was no exception, Philly realized in growing horror as light dawned. She was sitting at his feet, her heart pounding, her throat as dry as dust, gazing up at him as if he were the best thing to come along since double-Dutch chocolate ice cream. "Oh God!"

Beneath his thick mustache one corner of Morgan's mouth curled mockingly at her horrified whisper. "Not quite," he drawled. "Despite rumors to the contrary, I really can't walk on water."

He watched heat spill into her cheeks and temper into her sea green eyes and found himself transfixed. He'd spent most of the afternoon trying to convince himself that Philadelphia O'Neil couldn't possibly be as delicate as she'd appeared at the ridiculous press conference she'd called. The television cameras had obviously softened her features, somehow managing to give her a look of innocence that couldn't be real. But now, seeing her in person for the first time, her hair tumbling around her shoulders in artless disarray, her cheeks bright with embarrassment as she gracefully struggled to her feet without releasing the dog she still held trapped in her arms, he wasn't so sure.

And that wasn't like him. He'd grown up in and around Washington in the company of politicians. He'd learned at an early age not to be taken in by the obvious . . . the smile that came too easily and never reached the eyes, the handshake that disguised a stab in the back. Philadelphia O'Neil might look as sweet and innocent as cotton candy, but her sudden appearance, not only in his life, but Gussy's as well, was a hell of a coincidence. And he was a man who didn't believe in chance.

"Morgan!" With a cry of surprised delight, Gussy hurried into the entrance hall to give him a fierce hug. "I'm so glad you're here. Now you can finally meet Philly." Quickly performing the introductions, she chuckled. "You wouldn't believe what's been happening here! Philly brought some friends home with her and Mighty Mouse has thoroughly embarrassed himself—"

For the first time Morgan noticed the family of strangers that had clamored down the stairs at full tilt, only to stop at the sight of him. Their clothes were worn and thin, the boys' faded jeans patched many times over as they hid behind their parents. Morgan's narrowed gaze swung to Philly.

Philly told herself she didn't owe him any explanations, then could have kicked herself when she found herself giving him one anyway. "The shelter was full and the Cartwrights had nowhere else to go. They're staying with me tonight."

The lift of her chin dared him to argue with her. Regality wasn't something he'd expected from her, especially when she was still holding a wriggling dog that was nearly half as big as she was. He felt the pull of attraction, annoyingly strong, and bit back a curse, reminding himself why he was there. Deliberately he turned his attention to his grandmother. "I need to talk to you. And Ms. O'Neil."

His tone was grim, but Gussy only patted his shoulder and gave him a serene smile. "In a minute, dear. First we have to get the Cartwrights settled. Fix yourself a drink. We'll be right back." She swept out without a backward glance, the motley entourage that followed her brought up at the rear by Philly, who gave him a smile guaranteed to set his teeth on edge. With a muttered curse, he headed for the bar in the den. Gussy was right. He needed a drink.

By the time they returned, he was halfway through a Scotch and water and pacing the floor. At the sight of Philadelphia following Gussy into the den, her rounded chin still set at that damnably superior angle, he set his glass down with a snap. "I think it's time you started looking for another place to live, Ms. O'Neil," he said flatly. "The garage apartment is no longer appropriate for you."

Gussy looked at him as if he'd lost his mind. "Morgan! What on earth has gotten into you speaking to Philly like that? I've never known you to be so rude. Apologize to her."

But he only glanced at Philly with a challenging lift of his brow. "Are you going to tell her or shall I?"

Truly perplexed, not only by the question but also by the banked fury that seethed in his eyes, she spread her hands helplessly. Surely he couldn't be this enraged over a simple dare to work at the shelter! "I don't know what you're talking about."

"Oh, please, save me the sweetness-and-light act," he pleaded with a pained expression. "It's wasted on me. I already know you're working for King. All I have to do is prove it."

"*What?*"

"Why, that's ridiculous!" Gussy retorted indignantly. "Philly wouldn't lower herself to even talk to a scumbucket like Hollis King, let alone work for him."

Morgan never took his gaze from Philly's stunned face. "I don't know how she bamboozled you, Gus, but you obviously haven't been reading the papers. Ms. O'Neil isn't the innocent you think she is. While she's been living here, pretending to be your friend, she's been attacking my stand on the homeless in the paper with King's own words. Thanks to her, he's almost caught up with me in the polls. Then today—"

"She challenged you to work at the shelter," his grandmother finished for him. "Yes, I know. I suggested it."

For a minute he couldn't believe he'd heard her correctly. "You *what?*"

"I suggested it." She smiled at his startled expression and handed him his drink. "Don't look so shocked, dear. I'm on the board of directors of the

Franklin Shelter, and I'm well aware of what Philly's been doing because I've encouraged her every step of the way. *You're* the one I'm worried about.''

"Me—"

"Yes, you. King could have talked until he was blue in the face without ever gaining on you in the polls if he hadn't struck a nerve with some people. I know you care about people and your record in Congress reflects that, but you've obviously got some constituents who are afraid you can't relate to the problems of the average man who works hard just to survive. This will give you a chance to prove to them that you do.''

"It will also give you a chance to see the faces of the people you're going to vote to put back on the street," Philly taunted. "It'll be good for you."

Morgan sent her a glittering look. "Don't push me, Ms. O'Neil. You may have convinced Gussy of your innocence, but I still don't trust you as far as I can throw you."

Not the least disturbed by his hostility, Gussy only laughed, her faded blue eyes dancing. For too many years Morgan had dated only cool, sophisticated women who were more interested in his money and position than the man himself. Philly, however, wasn't impressed with either of those things and had already proven she wouldn't hesitate to bring him down a notch or two when she felt he was in the wrong. He needed that. And Philly needed someone to stir up her life, to give her something else to think about besides the shelter. At her age, she should have been pouring her heart and soul into a relationship instead of into her work.

"You two are going to be *so* good for each other!" she said happily. "I'm so glad I finally got you together." Beaming at their startled faces, she headed for the kitchen. "While you're getting acquainted, I'm going to find Mighty Mouse. He won't speak to me for a week if I don't soothe his ruffled feathers."

Horrified, Philly watched her glide out like a ship under full sail, leaving in her wake a mortifyingly awkward silence. Had Gussy just implied what she thought she'd implied? That she hadn't been planning to get them together to iron out their differences about the shelter funding bill, but because she wanted to get them *together?* Oh God, how could she have done this to her?

Her cheeks burning, she forced herself to look Morgan straight in the eye. "I—I'm sorry. I can't imagine where she got the idea that I ... that we ..."

He merely lifted a brow, his dark blue eyes fixed on her with an intensity that seemed to see into her very soul. She seemed truly shocked by Gussy's matchmaking scheme, but that might not mean anything other than that she was a damn fine actress. "Can't you?" he mocked, making no attempt to hide his suspicions. "You wouldn't be the first woman to make friends with her so you could chase me."

"Chase you!" If she hadn't been so surprised by the accusation, she would have laughed in his face. He couldn't be serious! She was hardly the femme-fatale type and couldn't even remember the last time she'd had a date. "You actually think I'm interested in you? That all my letters and phone calls were nothing but a plot to get your attention?"

He shrugged indifferently, his eyes watching her like those of a hawk. "I don't know. You tell me. If you're not working for King, then it's a logical assumption."

A low burn sparked to life deep inside her. Of all the unmitigated gall! Without so much as a by-your-leave, he dismissed her concerns for the homeless as if they were nothing to be taken seriously. How dare he! And then to assume that she was after him...wanted him.... Outrage nearly strangled her. Talk about ego! Granted, he was one of the most eligible bachelors around, and Gussy had told her tales of the women who had plotted and schemed to meet him, but she wasn't one of them. He might be God's gift to every other single woman in the state, but all she wanted from him was his support of the funding bill.

She opened her mouth to tell him just that, only to shut it with a snap, sudden mischief sparkling in her eyes. No, denying it wouldn't do any good. Maybe she needed to show him. Giving in to impulse, she stepped toward him, a half smile flirting with her mouth. Anyone who knew her well would have taken one look at the temper seething in her eyes and run for cover, but Morgan didn't have that advantage. He stood his ground, warily watching her approach. Stopping only inches away from him, her gaze boldly met his. "There seems to be a misunderstanding here that needs to be cleared up before we work together," she said softly.

He didn't move so much as a muscle when she reached out to teasingly finger his tie, but Philly would have sworn he stiffened. The finely drawn lines of his face implacably set, he stared down at her with shuttered eyes. "Oh? And what's that?"

"If I were to ever chase a man, there are a hundred ways I'd let him know I was interested in him," she whispered. "Like touching." With painstaking slowness, she trailed her finger up his tie to the collar of his shirt, to the warm skin just below his ear. She watched his eyes narrow and darken and should have felt some measure of satisfaction. But all she could feel was the sudden surprised pounding of her own heart and the trembling that seemed to start deep inside her, sending waves of heat rippling through her.

Stop! The warning rang in her ears. Morgan Stewart was not a man to be touched lightly, but she'd come too far to call a halt now. She had something to prove to him. And to herself. Lifting her hand to his mouth, she dared to trace the full, sensuous line of his lower lip. "If I were chasing you, I wouldn't hesitate to do this," she said, cursing the revealing huskiness of her voice. "But just for the record, that's not what I'm doing. I'm walking away." She dropped her hand to her side and summoned every ounce of control she possessed to give him a cool smile. "Good night, Congressman. Pleasant dreams."

Three

She must have been out of her mind.

Slumped at her desk, surrounded by paperwork she couldn't even bring herself to look at, Philly didn't even have to close her eyes to find herself back in Gussy's den, coming on to Morgan Stewart like a streetwalker in need of rent money. She'd blown it, she thought with a groan. Totally and completely blown it. How could she have been so stupid? He'd walked in already suspecting the worst of her, and her outrageous behavior had only confirmed his fears.

Damn her impulsiveness! When was she going to learn to control it? From early childhood, it had been the bane of her existence, the one character trait that had driven her usually calm, peace-loving parents right up the wall. They'd warned her that she couldn't keep throwing caution to the wind without one day paying a price for it, but she hadn't listened. And now the cost of her rashness just might be Morgan's support on the funding bill.

"You've really done it this time, Philly," she muttered to herself. She'd known before she'd ever laid eyes on him last night that it was going to take all her diplomatic skills just to work with him, let alone win him over to her side, so what had she done? She'd deliberately teased and infuriated him, then walked away with a proud tilt to her head.

And all the while her knees had been shaking and her insides melting with what she was horribly afraid had been desire.

She winced, rubbing at the headache that pounded in her head like a jackhammer. She must have been mistaken. She had to be. She had nothing in common with Morgan Stewart. He was a politician, for goodness' sake! He and his cohorts in Congress made her life miserable with paperwork and red tape when all she wanted to do was give people on the streets a warm place to sleep when they were cold and food to eat when they were hungry. What could she possibly want with a man like that? He already had more women than he knew what to do with and lived a life-style that was as foreign to her as Kansas was to Oz. He hadn't accepted her challenge to work at the shelter because of any sudden change of heart or a newly discovered concern for those who were without hope. He'd simply do anything to get reelected. Even work with her.

She couldn't allow herself to forget that.

Beside her the phone rang, jerking her back to the job at hand. Thankful for any distraction, she reached for it. "Franklin Shelter. This is Philadelphia O'Neil. May I help you?"

"You already have, Ms. O'Neil," a vaguely familiar voice purred in her ear. "I just wanted to congratulate you on taking Morgan Stewart down a peg or two."

She frowned, the satisfaction in the man's voice sending a chill sliding down her spine. "Who is this?"

"Hollis King," he replied with a chuckle. "We haven't had a chance to meet yet, but don't think I'm not aware of what you've been doing for me. You've been a big help."

Dismayed, Philly nearly dropped the phone. How had he gotten the impression that she was working for him? "Mr. King, there seems to be a misunderstanding here—"

"You know, it isn't often that a candidate can claim supporters in the enemy camp," he continued smugly, cutting her off. "You must be one cunning lady. I'd love to hear how you talked Augusta Stewart into letting you live with her. From what I've heard about the old broad, she's one tough nut to crack."

Philly gasped, outraged. How could this . . . sleaze actually think she endorsed him? She might not agree with Morgan on some issues, but she had never once doubted his integrity. He had one of the best reputations in Washington. Hollis King, however, was another matter. He was a smooth-talking, self-serving opportunist who would say whatever people wanted to hear in order to get to the top.

"That *old broad*, as you call her, happens to be a friend of mine," she said icily. "I wouldn't dream of discussing her or her grandson with you."

"But I thought—"

"It's obvious what you thought, Mr. King, but you thought wrong. I'm not one of your supporters. I won't take advantage of my position in the Stewart household to spy for you. Now if you'll excuse me, I have work to do."

She hung up abruptly, curtailing his squawking protest. Her face pale, she stared at the phone, Morgan's accusations from the night before echoing in her ears. How had this happened? she wondered. She wasn't a political person; she had little time to worry about what was going on on the Hill unless it directly affected the shelter. When she'd questioned Morgan about his stand on the homeless, she hadn't given the upcoming elections a second thought. Just that easily, she'd played right into his opponent's hands. No wonder Morgan was furious with her.

Unable to sit still, she got up to pace, her thoughts churning. She had to apologize, she decided. Her conscience wouldn't let her do anything else. When he came in later for his first evening of volunteer work, she would find a way to make him understand that helping King had never been her intention. She didn't delude herself into thinking he'd make it easy for her. Why should he? She had deliberately come on to him and antagonized him. She wouldn't blame him if he made her eat crow. Lord, she was dreading it.

Her mind made up, she went back to her paperwork, determined not to give Morgan Stewart another thought until he walked into the shelter at six o'clock. But the hours between afternoon and evening dragged in spite of the fact that she had more than enough work to keep her busy. Gussy called with the news that she'd found the Cartwright family an apartment in Arlington and both parents jobs with an old family friend. Once again memories of the night stirred, refusing to be repressed. Every time she unconsciously dropped her guard, she could almost feel Morgan's presence at her side, his fathomless blue eyes watching her, disturbing her, shooting her concentration straight to hell. When she should have been fine-tuning a new fund-raising plan, she found herself mulling over what she was going to say to him, wondering if she'd misjudged him. Had she been too harsh, too quick to lump him with every other aggrandizing politician she'd ever met simply because his views on the homeless differed so drastically from hers?

The thought nagged at her for hours. Then, before she was ready for the confrontation to come, evening was there and so was he. He couldn't have arrived at a worse time. Half the kitchen help was at home with the flu, dinner was late and she had her hands full trying to console a colicky baby whose teenage mother wasn't much more than a baby herself. Frazzled, murmuring softly to the baby as she paced, she turned and found herself trapped in the heat of his gaze as he walked through the front door.

For one timeless moment she saw nothing but him, heard nothing but the erratic skip of her heart pulsing in her ears. He'd obviously come straight from his office. Dressed in a navy blue, tailor-made suit and Italian leather shoes, he could have easily just stepped out of the pages of *GQ*. Philly tried to tell herself he looked reserved, aloof, unapproachable. But without any conscious thought on her part, her eyes lifted to his mouth, to the thick, enticing sweep of his dark mustache, to the tempting lower lip that she'd dared to touch. Just that quickly, the memory of how she had teased him was there in both their eyes, setting the air between them sizzling.

A movement behind him caught her attention, jerking her back to her surroundings. Her gaze moved past him and she saw what she should have seen the moment he stepped through the door—the crowd of reporters and cameramen swarming in after him. She stiffened. What a fool she was, she thought in disgust as the last, lingering hope that she had misjudged him fizzled and died. She'd informed no one that he intended to start his volunteer work tonight, so the press was obviously there at his invitation. He could talk until he was blue in the face about how much he cared about the poor, the homeless and the forgotten segments of society, but he was there for only one reason. To generate votes.

Too late, she realized the next five nights were going to be nothing but a farce. He would play the game, volunteer his time, and never see any of the faces of the people who needed him, never hear any of the cries of the children who were dragged from pillar to post by parents aimlessly roaming the streets, the country, looking for someone to turn to for help.

Disappointment she refused to acknowledge squeezed her heart, while all thought of apologizing died a swift death. Damn him, she wasn't going to let him get away with it! She wouldn't let him miss what was right beneath his nose.

Marching over to him, she ignored the reporters that eagerly awaited her reaction to his arrival and the cameras that were recording her every move. "I'm glad you're here," she said coolly. "We're short-handed tonight and Gary needs my help in the kitchen. While I'm doing that, you can watch Jenny for a while. She's got the colic and her mother's beat from walking the floor with her for the last two nights." Without another word of warning, she thrust the whining baby gently into his arms, making sure he had a firm hold on her and supported her head before she withdrew her hands.

Stunned, Morgan stared at the baby in horror as the cameras zoomed in. "Wait!" he cried in alarm when Philly turned toward the kitchen. "You can't just leave me like this! I don't know anything about babies. What do I do? She's crying."

If he expected sympathy, he didn't get it. "Cradle her against your chest and pat her. She just needs to know somebody cares."

Shooting him a speaking glance, she left him flustered and out of his depth, resenting the censure he'd seen in her eyes and the guilt she so easily stirred in him. Did she think he'd wanted to arrive like a fighter surrounded by his entourage? he thought irritably. His involvement with different charities was something he did privately, without fanfare or recognition. He'd have preferred to have kept it that way, but Tim had convinced him that was impossible. She was the one who had taken their disagreement public. She was the one who had forced him out onto center stage. She had no right to complain now that the eyes of the world were watching.

In his arms the baby let out a thin, mewling cry that went straight to his heart. Panic streaked through him as his arms compulsively tightened around the tiny bundle. That only turned her whimpering into an out-and-out scream of protest. His gaze jerked up to the reporters that all but surrounded him. "What'd I do?"

"Maybe you're squeezing her too tight," Mark Potts, a stringer for the *Baltimore Sun*, suggested. "If she's got the colic, her tummy hurts."

Morgan immediately loosened his hold, the worried frown grooving his forehead gradually easing as the baby's cries lessened to a fitful whine. Surprised, he shot the balding, potbellied reporter a suspicious look. "Potts, you old bachelor, where'd you learn about babies? I didn't think you'd know one end from the other."

The other man grinned crookedly. "Hey, I'm an uncle. I know about these things."

"So what do I do next?"

"Don't ask me," he said, laughing and backing away as if he was afraid Morgan would hand the baby to him at any moment. "That's the sum total extent of my knowledge. You're on your own, Congressman."

Jenny, however, thankfully solved the problem by drifting into sleep, her little mouth silently sucking.

Relieved, Morgan let out the breath he hadn't even realized he'd been holding and quickly looked around for a baby bed, but there wasn't one in sight. A young girl with eyes the color and shape of the baby's, however, suddenly appeared at his side and said quietly, "I'll take her now, sir. I'm her mother."

She couldn't have been a day over fifteen. Shock rippled through Morgan, followed by a blast of anger that he just barely controlled. Ever mindful of the watchful eye of the cameras present, his expression didn't alter by so much as a flicker of an eyelash, but inside he was seething. Where the hell were her parents, her family? he wanted to ask her. She was just a kid herself and had no business being in a place like this alone. She should be home, going to ball games and dances and falling in love with a different boy every other week.

But all he said was, "You have a beautiful baby. Thank you for letting me hold her."

She gave him a shy smile and retreated to the other room, and suddenly Morgan knew he'd had enough. He didn't give a damn what Tim or anyone else thought, the people who turned to the shelter for help had a right to their privacy. If he couldn't win the election without exploiting someone who was down on their luck, then it wasn't worth winning. Let King have it.

"Okay, boys, that's it. The show's over. Time for you to find yourself some real news to cover."

"You gotta be kidding!"

"We've hardly gotten anything at all—"

His jaw set, he stared them down. "Either you go or I do, it's that simple. I can always come back another time, when I'm sure there won't be any cameras present."

He'd do it, too, and they knew it. Grumbling and complaining, a few persistently tossing questions at him in spite of his stony glare, they headed for the door. Morgan was already striding toward the swinging door that led to what he presumed was the kitchen before they even stepped outside.

He found Philly pulling cobblers from the ovens of the commercial stoves that formed a work center in the middle of the long, oblong room, while two men quickly transferred hot food from the stoves to the steam tables in the dining room. Her cheeks stained red from the heat, she'd wrapped herself in a huge apron that all but swallowed her petite figure and should have looked ridiculous. Instead it only seemed to emphasize the narrow span of her waist and the sweet, tempting curve of breasts that were all but hidden from view.

Morgan almost walked out then and there. The woman was a constant thorn in his side, an irritant that refused to go away. She had an uncanny knack for annoying the hell out of him and making his blood heat at one and the same time, and he wanted nothing more to do with her. He'd put in an appearance. He could leave now and no one would be the wiser. The evening news would show his arrival at the shelter; tomorrow a picture of him holding the baby would no doubt be splashed across the front page. Tim would be happy, the reporters would have their copy, and he would show the green-eyed little witch across the room that he wasn't a man she could play games with.

It should have been that simple. But from the very first moment he'd seen her on TV, her eyes impudently daring him, nothing had been simple. As surely as he knew that he could pull out this election, he knew she was trouble, the kind he'd avoided all his life. A wise man would have cut and run hard and fast in the opposite direction. No one was more surprised—or exasperated—than he was when he took a step toward her.

"You look like you could use some help."

Startled, Philly forced herself not to look up from the cobbler she'd just removed from the oven. She'd heard the reporters leave and had assumed he had, too. After all, he'd gotten what he'd come for, hadn't he? So why was she so upset? Setting the heavy baking dish down on top of the stove with a clatter, she turned to face him, her balled hands planted on her hips. "You got the publicity you came for. I thought you'd left."

She was foot-stomping, eyes-flashing mad, spoiling for a fight, and too damn beautiful for words. Caught flat-footed, Morgan felt a stronger, deeper tug of attraction and wanted to curse. Scowling, he stayed right where he was. "And give you the satisfaction of thinking the worst of me?" he retorted. "Not on your life, lady. And before you start calling the pot black, you'd better take a good, hard look at yourself. I didn't use the press until you did." When she opened her mouth only to shut it again, he lifted a sardonic brow. "You were saying?"

What could she say? Blast the man, he was right!
"But I only used it to get your attention—"

"Believe me, you got it," he cut in dryly, letting his
gaze drop down to her mouth before snapping back up
to her eyes. "Now that we've got that cleared up, don't
you think it's time we tried to find a way to get along?
We're going to be working together for five nights. I
don't know about you, but I'd like to get through it
with my skin and bones still intact."

She didn't want to relax the hostilities between
them, didn't want any reason to like him. But she said,
grudgingly, "We'll need some help serving. And you'd
better get out of that suit coat before you ruin it. I'll
get you an apron."

As far as truces went, it wasn't much. But Morgan
had worked in Congress long enough to recognize a
peace offering when he saw one. Fighting back a smug
grin, he slipped out of his jacket. "Whatever you say.
You're the boss."

His self-satisfied good humor, however, lasted no
longer than the time it took for her to grab an apron
identical to hers from a hook near the back door. Instead of being halfway across the room from him, she
was suddenly slipping around behind him as he pulled
the apron over his head, obviously intending to tie it
for him. He knew by the casual way she reached for
the strings that she did it without thought, but the instant her hands brushed the sides of his waist, tension
thickened the air between them.

Morgan went perfectly still, his jaw rigid, his eyes
trained unseeingly on the cobblers cooling on the stove
as teasing, unbidden images played on his mind. Philly

standing too close. Her breasts only a whisper away from his back. Her fingers reaching to explore him.

You've been too long without a woman, Stewart, he told himself in disgust. *It's time you got off the campaign trail and found yourself some female companionship. And I don't mean Philadelphia O'Neil! A bleeding heart liberal with a cause is the last thing you need.*

Staring at his stiff back, Philly dropped her gaze to fingers that suddenly couldn't manage to tie a simple bow. This is crazy! she told herself. Morgan Stewart was going to be in her life for exactly five days and no longer, and that was just the way she wanted it. It wasn't like her to get all hot and bothered over a man she hardly knew, especially one like Morgan who could never, under any circumstances, be right for her. Why, then, couldn't she shake the knowledge that if she moved her hand just an inch, she could test the unyielding strength of his spine?

Snatching her hands back as if she'd been scorched, she sent up a silent prayer of thanks that he couldn't see the burning brilliance of her cheeks. "There, you're all ready," she said with false brightness. Avoiding his gaze, she moved toward the swinging door that led to the serving line that occupied one wall of the dining room. "Come on, I'll introduce you to my assistant and the other volunteer who will be helping you serve. While they're showing you the ropes, I'll open the doors to the dining room before someone decides to break them down. We're running horribly late."

That was the last time they came close to each other all evening.

She was avoiding him, deliberately finding tasks that took her to other parts of the shelter for long stretches at a time. Morgan knew it, accepted it, thanked God for it. Out of sight, he could forget the way her green eyes snapped fire at him, the way his fingers itched to encircle her wrist just to see if her bones were as delicate as they looked, the way her clean, fresh scent seemed to linger in the air long after she'd moved out of reach. In fact, he wouldn't voice a word of complaint if he didn't see hide nor hair of her for the next five nights. A man couldn't be tempted by what he couldn't see.

Satisfied he'd banished her to the back of his mind, he turned his attention to his surroundings. What he saw disturbed him. Philly and the rest of the staff had done everything possible to make the shelter as homey as possible, but bright curtains on the windows and toy boxes full of used toys for the kids couldn't make it a home. Despair was everywhere...in the tired droop of mothers' shoulders as they watched their children play with sad, dull eyes...in the beaten, defeated faces of men who were still in their prime but unable to support their families simply because there was no place for them in the work force.

He clenched his jaw at the injustice of it, and by the end of his four-hour shift, he was more convinced than ever that these people needed jobs, not more shelters. They needed their pride back, their self-worth restored, and that could only be done by giving them the training they needed to earn their own way. He almost sought Philly out to tell her that as he shrugged into his coat, but it would have destroyed the truce they'd managed to achieve. Tomorrow would be soon enough to warn her that her plans were backfiring in her face.

Keeping his distance, his gaze met hers across the width of the lounge. Something—heat, a silent meeting and touching of souls—passed between them. Oddly shaken, he fought the urge to cross to her. He nodded stiffly instead, then turned abruptly on his heel and left.

The minute he stepped out of the warmth of the shelter, silence slammed into him, then the cold. Lifting his face to the night, he dragged in a bracing breath, welcoming it. Anything to get his mind off the woman he'd had to force himself to walk away from. His dark brows met in a deep V over the bridge of his nose at the thought. Sometime between now and tomorrow night when he saw her again, he was going to have to come to grips with his body's unwanted reaction to her, but for now, he just wanted to clear his mind and walk.

Turning up his collar against the seeking, restless fingers of the wind, he buried his hands in his pockets and headed for his car, the echo of his footsteps a hollow cadence that followed him in the dark. The streets were dark and hostile, and he'd parked two blocks away in the only parking space he'd been able to find. Increasing his pace, his guarded eyes hopscotched from black, shadowed doorways to even blacker alleys, on the alert for the trouble he could almost smell in the air.

But nothing moved save a cat scrounging in a Dumpster and with a sigh of relief he turned the corner to where he'd left his car. Two steps later he stopped dead in his tracks, cursing furiously. The black BMW was still there, right where he'd left it. But it wasn't going anywhere. Someone had set it up on apple crates and stolen the tires.

Philly had just locked up her office and bid Gary good-night when Morgan stormed back into the shelter, his dark hair practically standing on end from the force of the wind, his blue eyes blazing as he strode over to the registration desk and reached for the phone. Alarmed, she hurried toward him. "Morgan! What is it? What's wrong? Who are you calling?"

Livid, he hardly noticed that this was the first time she'd called him by his name. "The police," he bit out through clenched teeth, jabbing 9-1-1. "And a wrecker. Some jackass stole the tires off my BMW."

"Off your..." Her voice trailed off into a hastily swallowed gurgle of amusement. He couldn't have, she thought, fighting a grin. He couldn't have left a Beamer unattended in this neighborhood! Her hand at her throat to hold back the laughter bubbling up inside her, she struggled to look properly horrified. "Was, ah, anything else taken?"

"No." His gaze narrowed at the sight of her dancing eyes, but the 911 operator came on the line just then, distracting him. As soon as he finished reporting the incident and hung up, however, his eyes swung back to the woman at his side, pinning her there. "Have I said something to amuse you? Because if I have, I wish you'd tell me what it is. I could use a good laugh right about now."

He gave her a glare that would have sent a House page scurrying for cover. Far from being intimidated, Philly only shook her head, then nearly bent double with eye-watering laughter. Gussy was right. He really did take himself entirely too seriously. "It's nothing...r-really."

In spite of himself, Morgan couldn't stop his lips from twitching. Little witch! "I know I was a fool to leave it on the street, but where else was I supposed to park it?"

"In the lot behind the shelter," she explained, struggling for control. "That's where I always park my Lamborghini."

She dissolved into fresh chuckles, utterly destroying the last of his anger. Staring down at her, unable to drag his gaze away, he knew he was in trouble. A woman who held her own with him in a battle of wits was one to be respected. But one who could make him laugh when the car he loved had been stripped down to the hubs was far too dangerous for his peace of mind.

Turning back to the phone abruptly, he snatched up the receiver as if it were a lifeline. "The cops'll be here soon. I'd better call the auto club and see about a taxi."

"I'll take you home."

The hasty words popped out before she could stop them, then just hung there between them in the sudden loud silence. Philly tried to tell herself she'd only made the offer because she felt responsible—after all, he never would have stepped foot in this part of the city if it hadn't been for her. And for the span of a heartbeat she almost believed it, but she'd never been very good at lying to herself. Like it or not she wanted to spend more time with him. Had she lost her mind?

Her cheeks stinging, she said hastily, "Of course, if you'd rather take a cab, it's no big deal. It's late, the Lamborghini's not even warmed up. Sometimes she can be temperamental and you've already been stranded once tonight. Twice in one evening is more than anyone deserves—"

"Philadelphia."

He only had to say her name in that low sexy way of his to steal her breath. She swallowed. "Yes?"

"Why don't you warm up the Lamborghini while we're waiting for the cops? Then she'll be ready when we are."

Four

The heater of her VW Bug blowing nothing but cold air, Philly watched Morgan cram all six feet of his lean body into the seat next to her and could have sworn the temperature in the compact car rose twenty degrees. Her heart fluttering in her breast, she unconsciously rubbed damp palms against the steering wheel. This was a mistake! she thought wildly. The car was too small, he was too big, and there was just no way to ignore his nearness. Drawn to the long length of his legs, her eyes dropped to where his left knee rested only inches away from the gearshift. She wouldn't even be able to shift without brushing her fingers against him. She could already feel the heat from the innocent contact shooting up her arm.

"How long does it take to warm her up?"

Startled, her eyes flew to his. "I beg your pardon?"

"The Lamborghini," he explained, his smile flashing teasingly in the darkness as he rubbed his hands together briskly. "She's been idling for fifteen minutes. Doesn't she ever get hot?"

"Only in the middle of summer," she retorted dryly, reaching for the stick shift. "Hang on."

The warning was for her as much as it was for him. Bracing herself, she shifted into gear and tore out of the parking lot like a bat out of hell, her only thought to get him home as quickly as possible. At her side, Morgan swore and grabbed for the dash, drawing a laugh from her. But then she took a corner on what felt like two wheels and the force threw him toward her, his shoulder nudging hers. In less time than it took to blink, the laughter fell from her face and her breath lodged in her throat. Suddenly the car was smaller than before, the air warmer and humming with expectation, their bodies too close. Keeping her eyes trained straight ahead, she tried desperately not to notice.

That was when she saw them. A group of men camped on a grate on a corner, the plastic they'd wrapped themselves in and the steam that rose through the metal grillwork they sat on their only protection against the icy coldness of the night. As she sped past them, the man nearest the curb held up a roughly written cardboard sign: Will Work For Food.

The words went through Philly like a hot bullet, tearing at her, and she never noticed how still and silent Morgan had become next to her. No matter how many times she saw proud men reduced to begging on the streets, she couldn't get used to it. Couldn't accept it. She knew some of them were there of their own choice. Hard-edged loners who wanted nothing to do with society, they actually welcomed the isolation and hardships of homelessness. But it was the others, the ones who were given no choice, that broke her heart. They were the ones slipping through the cracks when no one seemed to notice. She couldn't just drive by them and pretend they didn't exist.

Up ahead a Kentucky Fried Chicken sign shone like a beacon in the night. Never one to question the vagaries of Fate, she made a sudden, sharp turn into the nearly empty parking lot.

Morgan glanced at her in surprise. "What's this? A pit stop?"

Cutting the engine, she reached for her purse. "I won't be but a minute. I'm going to get a bucket and take it back to those men."

Morgan couldn't have been more shocked if she'd told him she was going to stand on her head and stack BB's. "You can't be serious!"

Her eyes narrowed at his tone. "And if I am? Those men are hungry."

"What they are is probably armed and dangerous and looking for a sucker to rob," he retorted. "Leave them alone before you find yourself in more trouble than you can handle."

Philly shot him a pitying look and pushed open her door. "If you think everyone who lives on the street is a criminal, Congressman, then it's no wonder you're against the funding bill. Gussy was right. Working at the shelter's going to be good for you."

"I never said—damn it, Philadelphia, get back in the car!"

But it was too late. Ignoring him she slammed the car door and sailed into the restaurant. It was the last straw. She had no right to throw such a ludicrous accusation at him just because he was cautious, Morgan fumed, glaring after her. Yes, there were innocent people forced to live on the streets, but there were thieves and crackheads and murderers, too. How could she work in one of the worst areas of the city and have no concept of its dangers? Cursing, he pushed open his door.

Her eyes on the menu, Philly could almost hear the grinding of Morgan's teeth as he joined her. Fighting a smile, she didn't spare him a glance. "Should we get one bucket or two? We wouldn't want anyone to go hungry."

We? he thought indignantly. When had he agreed to be a part of this madness? "Damn it, Philly, you're making a mistake!"

"Three, then?" she asked, widening her eyes innocently. "Do you really think so? That seems like an awful lot."

He was, Morgan decided dispassionately, going to strangle her. Conscious of the man behind the counter watching them with rapt interest, he leaned closer and hissed, "You're not going to make me the villain in this just because you don't have the sense to be leery of a gang of men hanging out on a dark street corner.

I'm not a monster, you know. I don't want to see any-one go hungry anymore than you do—''

"Good, because if we're going to buy three buck-ets, you're going to have to cough up some change. I've only got enough for two." Smiling sweetly, as if he'd just reaffirmed her faith in him, she held out her hand, palm up.

Staring down at her, he fought the sudden insane urge to reach for her, to close his fingers over hers and drag her against him and taste the honeyed recesses of her mouth. His face stony, he forced himself to reach for his wallet instead. "Here," he said flatly, handing her a twenty. "Buy the damn chicken. But if this blows up in our faces, you're never going to hear the end of this. You got that?"

Grinning, Philly snatched the bill out of his hand. "Got it!"

Five minutes later, loaded down with the chicken and enough biscuits to feed a small army, they raced back to the corner where the men still huddled on the grate. Before Philly had set the brake, Morgan was opening his door. "You stay here. I'll take care of this."

She only laughed and pocketed her keys. "You re-ally do need to lighten up, Congressman. I'm not one of those helpless females who needs a man to protect her from the bogeyman. I know what I'm doing, who to trust, who to keep my distance from. This is my turf, remember?"

Morgan scowled. The message underlying her words was loud and clear. She might look like she was as soft as spun sugar, but she wasn't like the women in his world. She was streetwise and tough, and he'd do well to remember that. But that didn't mean he had to like standing by and watching her take chances. "Just be careful," he said harshly. "Okay? Is that too much to ask?"

He really was worried about her. The knowledge surprised her, warmed her, and made her want to run for cover. She was already attracted to him, she warned herself. She wouldn't, couldn't let herself like him. He was a card-carrying, dyed-in-the-wool conservative who had never known a day of want in his life. He had no concept of the world she lived in and was fighting to change. Then why did she find it so difficult to remember that?

"I'm always careful," she said quietly, and pushed open her door.

The men who warily watched them approach were a rough-looking group. There were five of them, tall as giants in the darkness, their black clothes blending into the night, their eyes shuttered. Nerves taut, Morgan hovered protectively at Philly's side. Whether she liked it or not, he was pushing her behind him at the first sign of trouble.

But it became clear almost immediately that that wouldn't be necessary. Philly strode forward with an easy, open smile and a gutsy courage that Morgan couldn't help but admire. Introducing herself as the director of the Franklin Shelter, she offered them the food, started chatting like they were old friends, and had them eating out of her hand in less than a minute. Morgan could only watch her and shake his head.

If she'd chosen to go into politics instead of social work, she'd have been hell on wheels.

"Hey, aren't you Morgan Stewart? The congressman?"

The question came from the oldest man in the group. Rail-thin and gaunt, he looked as if he should have been enjoying his retirement on a Florida beach somewhere instead of freezing on a northern street corner. Before Morgan could answer him, however, a scruffy blond hulk scoffed, "You need your glasses adjusted, Ford. Ain't Stewart one of those hoity-toity rich boys? What would he be doing out here in the cold with us?"

Philly stifled a giggle and lifted a brow at Morgan, daring him to answer that one. Shooting her a quelling frown, he drawled, "I wouldn't have described myself that way, but I am Morgan Stewart."

Whatever reaction Morgan had expected, it wasn't the one he got. After their initial exclamations of astonishment, the men pressed forward, everyone talking at once as they introduced themselves and threw surprisingly astute questions at him. Before he quite knew how it happened, he found himself in a political discussion on the pros and cons of increased defensive spending, considering the current world situation.

Philly loved it. *This* was what she'd hoped for when she'd challenged Morgan to come out of his safe, isolated world and onto the streets. These were people he was talking to, not statistics. Their voice was usually silent, unheard, but they had hopes and dreams just like the mainstream of society. If he was the man she thought he was, the man his grandmother swore would one day be every bit as great as his grandfather, then he would not only listen, he would hear.

Caught up in her musings, she didn't notice the older man who had first recognized Morgan watching her until he suddenly snapped his fingers. "Now I know who you are. I didn't make the connection before when you said you were with the shelter. You're the one who's been feuding with the Congressman in the papers."

"I guess that's one way of putting it," Philly said with a smile. "We've agreed to disagree."

"Ms. O'Neil's a liberal," Morgan put in. "You know how they are—they solve a problem by throwing money at it. If she had her way, we'd get the homeless off the streets by building new shelters all over the country."

"And what's wrong with that?" she demanded. "All you can think about is job training." She snorted. "It'll take years for those types of programs to make any measurable difference on the street people. What are they supposed to do in the meantime? Freeze?"

"I wouldn't be out here now if I had a job," one of the men said quietly.

"Me, either," another joined in. "But I ain't been able to find nothing since I got laid off."

"I hear they're hiring in Texas," the older man added. "But how the hell's an old man like me gonna get to Texas? Walk?"

Morgan merely looked at Philly without saying a word. From the light of a distant streetlight, she could just make out the satisfaction gleaming in his eyes. Surely he didn't think he'd won so easily? she thought, annoyed.

Turning to the older man, she said, "Lack of a job doesn't explain why you're out here tonight instead of in a shelter. I know some men would rather freeze than come in off the streets, but you guys don't seem the type. Why don't you go sign up for a bed and get out of the cold?"

"And take it from somebody who needs it more? No way, lady."

"No matter how bad we think we got it, there's always someone who's got it worse," the hulk agreed.

"Like the women and kids whose men have run out on them," came a disgusted voice from the back. "I may have lost my job, but I still got my self-respect. And no woman with a baby is going to sleep on a damn grate while I stretch out in a nice warm bed. It ain't gonna happen."

Vindicated, Philly glanced at Morgan without saying a word. What else was there to say? They were back to square one.

After that, there seemed little point in continuing the discussion. They graciously accepted the men's thanks for the food, declined the invitation to share it with them, then climbed back into the car without even looking at each other. Seconds later Philly shifted into first, eased up on the clutch and shot off toward Georgetown.

This time there were no jokes about her Lamborghini, no attempts at conversation, friendly or otherwise. They sat only inches apart, but it might as well have been miles. Careful not to touch, to even look at each other, they stared straight ahead as silence surrounded them like a fog.

But Philly didn't have to look at him to know his eyes were brooding, his face sober, his lean, athletic body stiff and unyielding. She tried to convince herself it was for the best. For a while there she'd made the mistake of forgetting that he was a man she couldn't allow herself to become interested in. He was too rich, too sophisticated, his philosophy on life the complete opposite of hers. His idea of charity was writing a check, hers was pushing up her sleeves and doing whatever needed to be done to help those in need. If nothing else, tonight had proved that they were, and probably always would be, at cross purposes about the things that meant the most to her. To think differently would only invite a heartache she didn't want or need.

"Turn right at the next corner. It's the second townhouse on the left."

His quiet words came out of the darkness like a caress, whispering over her, stirring her senses, making a mockery of all her fine resolves. Her fingers tight on the steering wheel, she struggled for control by recalling all the times she had seen Morgan's picture splashed across the society page, one beautiful, gorgeous, rich woman after another at his side. She wasn't part of that world and never would be, which was probably just as well, she thought ruefully. He'd been out with so many women that she doubted he remembered half of them, and she'd never been interested in being just another nameless face in the crowd.

Pulling over to the curb in front of a well-preserved yet elegant townhouse of weathered red brick and old brass, she shifted into neutral and turned slightly in her seat toward him. Her smile was too forced to be comfortable, but he would never know that in the darkness. "Well, Congressman, here you are," she said lightly. "All safe and sound and not a scratch on you, just as I promised."

He should have thanked her for the lift and gone inside right then and there. She wasn't a woman he wanted to linger in a car with, not after all the trouble she'd caused him during the last month. But instead of reaching for the door handle, he found himself remembering the feel of her finger tracing his mouth and the loud hammer of his heart echoing in his ears. No woman had ever stirred him so quickly, so hotly, with nothing more than the stroke of her fingers.

He had to have imagined it.

Even in the shadowy light, Philly could see him staring off into space, a glower of disapproval darkening his brow. Reaching across the space between them, she snapped her fingers directly in front of his nose. "Congressman? Morgan? Hey, are you in there?"

He blinked, grabbing at her hand before he gave himself time to think. Her startled eyes met his in the darkness, her nearly silent gasp as loud as a thunderclap in the sudden, utter stillness.

Let her go! a hoarse voice ordered deep inside him. *Now. Before you do something you'll regret.*

But he was mesmerized by the feel of her soft hand under his and a memory that wouldn't let him go. It was stupid, it was madness, but he had to know if it was the surprise of her unexpected caress or the woman herself he had responded to last night. As quickly as he'd grabbed her hand, he released it, but only to tunnel his fingers through the dark, tempting curls at her neck and abruptly drag her closer.

For a heartbeat, he held her there, his eyes full of fire, raging over her startled face in the poor light. If he'd seen fear there, he would have released her in an instant. But this was a woman who didn't know the meaning of the word. She met his warning look head-on, daring him. Cursing her, wanting her, he slammed his mouth over hers.

Even then, it should have been an easy kiss, one he could walk away from as effortlessly as she'd walked away from him last night. But the moment his lips touched hers, he knew nothing would ever be easy again.

Reason splintered and scattered at the feel of her, the taste of her. Small, he thought in confusion, tugging her closer in spite of the gearshift that separated them. When had she gotten so small, so dainty? The woman was the prizefighter of the underdogs, a female David undaunted by Goliath. She shouldn't feel so crushable in his arms. Or so sweet. Didn't she know what she was doing to him? He'd expected a struggle, at the very least a coldness that would freeze his blood. But she gave him heat instead, flames that crackled and popped and shot sparks into the darkness of his soul. Sinking fast into something he couldn't explain, he could only clutch at her, even then unable to release her.

Her mind reeling, Philly couldn't have managed a murmur of protest if she'd wanted to. She'd seen the intent in his eyes, the promise she'd refused to back away from. After tonight she knew she'd never again allow herself to be alone with him in a small, dark place, so what could one kiss hurt? She would satisfy her curiosity, see what all the fuss was about, then proceed to put the playboy congressman right out of her head.

When pigs flew.

Later she told herself she could have handled a deliberate seduction. But this . . . this was something out of the realm of her experience. Instead of the skill and finesse she'd braced herself for, he sent her spinning with a desperate hunger that seemed to stun him as much as it did her. At the nip of his teeth, she moaned, bones melting, clinging to reality by a thread. Then his tongue stole into her mouth like a secret lover, demanding a response she was helpless to refuse. Whimpering, she crowded closer, and never even knew when she turned soft and pliant and vulnerable in his arms.

Do you realize you're steaming up the windows with a man who only yesterday accused you of chasing him?

The dry observation made by the voice of reason ripped through her passion-clouded mind with all the subtlety of a chain saw. She stiffened, horrified. Dear God, what was she doing?

"No!"

"Philly! What the—"

Wrenching out of his arms, she scooted away from him, but her VW was hardly bigger than a sardine can and there was nowhere to go. Her mouth throbbing and body humming, she saw him blink as if he were just coming out of a fog, his hands already reaching for her. In the next instant she was out of the car and slamming her door behind her.

The night air stung her hot cheeks, and from inside the car she could hear Morgan's muttered curse. But she only bent her head and squeezed her eyes shut, closing him out as she tried to steady her still-ragged breathing. She never knew how long she stood there, her fingers curling against the cold roof of the car, but when she finally opened her eyes, he stood across from her, his dark gaze locked unwaveringly on her face. She hadn't even heard him get out of the car.

"Despite what just happened, I don't want you. I'm not a member of your fan club, and I'm not chasing you. You got that?"

Her voice was flat and cold as ice. Stunned by the strength of his need to go to her, to touch her, to drag her back into his arms and make a mockery of her denial, Morgan stood rooted to the spot, seething with a turmoil that both confused and irritated him. Who did she think she was kidding? He'd tasted the heat of her response and nearly been burned alive by it. The lady was *not* indifferent.

And neither was he.

His jaw clenched at the silent admission, his eyes hard. It'd been a long time since he'd nearly lost his head with a woman, and he didn't like it any better now than he had then. Cynthia. How could he have forgotten the lessons she'd taught him? He'd been young and stupid and in love for the first time in his life. He'd never stopped to question her fascination with his family money and power until it was almost too late. He'd been on the verge of asking her to marry him when he'd overheard her telling a girlfriend that once she hooked him, she'd be sitting pretty for the rest of her life and her family's money problems would be solved for good. Devastated, he had broken things off immediately and vowed that from then on, he'd enjoy women, but never again take one seriously unless she had nothing to gain from her involvement with him.

And Philadelphia O'Neil had more to gain than any woman he'd ever met. If he could just eliminate the distance between them and haul her back into his arms, he knew he could make her admit once and for all what she wanted from him. But he also might not be able to let her go.

A muscle ticked along his jaw at the thought. There were other, safer ways than touching her to get at the truth, other ways to expose her for what she really was.

"I got it," he said coolly. "My mistake. Let's just chalk it up to the lateness of the hour and a momentary loss of sanity and forget it. Okay?"

A laugh that came perilously close to a strangled sob threatened to choke her. Forget it? The taste of him would still be with her when she was a hundred and one! Struggling for control, she nodded stiffly. "I couldn't agree more. Now that we have that settled, I'd better go. Good night, Congressman."

Without a word, he stepped back from the curb, his hands balled in his pockets. Seconds later she was gone, the taillights of the Bug winking at him as she sped off into the night. Morgan told himself she couldn't drive out of his life fast enough to please him. But as he turned to walk into the house, his body was still hot for her in spite of the coldness of the night air. It was going to be a long night.

When the package arrived the next afternoon, Philly was in Gussy's kitchen sharing the latest gossip over pie and coffee before leaving to work the late shift. In actuality Gussy was the one doing the talking, gaily chattering on about the dinner party she'd gone to the night before. Normally Philly would have been chuckling over the older woman's sharp, pithy descriptions of D.C.'s movers and shakers, but today she couldn't seem to think of anything but Morgan. It'd been over twelve hours since she'd left him in her rearview mirror, determined to put him out of her head as easily as she'd floorboarded the accelerator and raced away from him. But he was still firmly entrenched, rising up to haunt her the second she let her thoughts stray.

At the sight of the delivery man standing on her doorstep with a small package addressed to Philly, Gussy sighed in relief. Maybe this would cheer the girl up. She'd spent the last fifteen minutes trying to draw a smile out of her, without success. What the devil had Morgan done to her? After spending the evening butting heads with him last night, she should have been ranting and raving about him the way she usually did. Instead she was quiet as a church mouse, and Gussy didn't like it. They were both stubborn, both volatile, both committed in their own ways to righting the wrongs of the world. After just one evening, they should have been striking sparks off each other. Something was wrong.

Signing for the package, she hurried back to the kitchen. "Did you order something? This just came for you." She held out the small paper-wrapped box to Philly, who looked at it in surprise but made no attempt to take it. "Go on," Gussy said, laughing. "Maybe it's from a secret admirer."

"Who?"

"Philly! Will you open it, for heaven's sakes? I'm dying of curiosity!"

For the life of her, Philly couldn't have explained her reluctance. She usually loved surprises, but there was something about this one that made her fingers tremble. Slowly reaching for it, she tore away the paper to free the small box inside. At the sight of the jeweler's box, her throat went dry. Holding her breath, she lifted the lid. And gasped.

There, on a bed of ivory satin, lay an antique gold bracelet of tiny, delicately worked roses.

Stunned, she could only stare at it while her heart hammered against her ribs. Biting her lower lip, she carefully pulled out the card that accompanied it and silently read: *I was going to send you flowers to apologize, but thought these would last longer.* There was no name, but she didn't need one. Only one man had a reason to apologize to her. Only one man could have such exquisite taste.

Her fingers crushing the card, she set the box down abruptly and replaced the lid, afraid she wouldn't be able to resist temptation if she didn't. Dear God, why couldn't he have sent her something frightfully gaudy? That she could have thrown back in his face. But this... She'd never seen anything so beautiful in her life, anything so perfectly suited to her. She ached to touch it, but didn't dare. How had he known?

"Well?" Gussy demanded, unable to bear the suspense another moment. "Who's it from?"

"Morgan."

Philly had expected her to react with smugness at the admission, at the very least, satisfaction that her plan to throw them together appeared to be working. But it was disapproval she saw in the older woman's eyes, that and a disappointment she made no attempt to hide. Alarmed, she said, "I hope you're not starting to think I'm chasing him, too. This whole challenge was your idea, Gussy. I'm not after your grandson!"

"I know that, dear, but evidently Morgan still doesn't trust you."

"What do you mean?"

"If he'd sent you something silly and inexpensive, I'd be thrilled. But this—" shaking her head, she opened the jeweler's box and sighed "—this isn't a sign that he's interested in you. It's too beautiful and expensive for that. I know Morgan. He's been hounded all his adult life by women who were more interested in what he could buy them than in him. If you accept this now, when you hardly know him, you'll be proving to him that you're just another greedy female out for what you can get.''

"My God, he's testing me!" Shocked Philly stared at the delicate piece of jewelry as if it were a snake waiting to strike, pain lancing her heart, surprising her, infuriating her. Making a snap decision, she snatched up the box, crammed the bracelet and card back inside and headed for the door.

Gussy jumped to her feet. "Where are you going?"

Philly didn't even break stride. "To tell your precious grandson exactly what I think of him!"

Five

—

Driving across town, she promised herself she wasn't going to loose her cool. She would be dignified, reserved, explicit, and never raise her voice. But the traffic was teeth-gnashingly slow and parking spaces as scarce as backers of a congressional pay raise during an election year by the time she finally reached Capitol Hill. It took her half an hour to find a meter, and it had a fifteen-minute limit. Five would have been enough. That's all it would take to tell him what a tricky, underhanded, suspicious snake he was.

By the time she charged up the steps of the Capitol, she'd worked up a full head of steam. The package clutched in her hand like a baseball she intended to bean him with, she found his office and strode inside, her green eyes blazing. Oh, she was going to enjoy this!

But the sight of his secretary, zealously guarding his domain, brought her up short. Her gaze dropped to the nameplate on her desk, but she already knew who she was. Mary Barker. The dragon who screened his calls and mail and protected him from the constant demands on his time. After numerous run-ins with her on the phone, Philly would have sworn she was as big as a Marine and twice as tough. Instead she looked like a frail sparrow with glasses as she perched behind the desk, nearly lost behind the mountain of files piled before her.

The moment Philly saw her perceptive brown eyes, she knew she was nobody's fool. Mary Barker might not be as big as a wren, but her gaze was straight and direct and sharp with recognition. Philly wasn't surprised that she recognized her. The older woman was the kind of secretary who would make it a point to know not only Morgan's friends, but anyone who represented a threat to him, as well.

Squaring her shoulders, Philly said, "I need to see the Congressman."

Mary didn't bother to ask if she had an appointment—she knew she didn't. "He's very busy, Ms. O'Neil. May I ask what this is about? Maybe I can help you."

Holding up the box that contained the bracelet, she glared at it disdainfully. "It's about this... trinket I received this afternoon. And no, you can't help me, thank you. What I have to say has to be said in person."

Mary's polite, but reserved expression immediately iced over. She knew of only one woman who would describe a five-hundred dollar bracelet as a "trinket." Cynthia. "It's not enough?"

Confused, Philly drew back as if the woman were speaking to her in pig latin. "Not enough? Good Lord, of course it's enough. It's *too* much! It must have cost the earth."

The older woman merely lifted a brow. "You don't like it? You can return it, of course, and get something of equal value. The Congressman suggested something delicate, but I didn't know your taste...."

Philly stood as if turned to stone, the hurt that had driven her to confront him nothing compared to the pain that now squeezed her heart. It had been bad enough when she'd realized the insult behind the gift. But he hadn't even cared enough to do the dirty work himself! He'd left it to this secretary!

Hot tears, unexpected and thick, welled in her throat and threatened to do the same in her eyes. Horrified, she blinked rapidly, forcing them back, her fingers so tight on the package she almost crushed it. She would not cry! she promised herself fiercely, but it was a long, tense moment before she could force any words between her tightly clenched teeth. "You don't understand, Mrs. Barker. I don't want anything from Congressman Stewart. Nothing. Nada. I wouldn't even stop him on the street to ask him the time of day."

Startled, Mary could only stare at her. "Oh."

"So if you'll just point me in the direction of his office, I'll return his property to him and tell him exactly that," she continued in a voice that grew progressively stronger and colder. "I'm sure he'll be relieved to hear it."

During her long years of service with the Stewart men, Mary had seen her share of irate constituents. But she'd never seen one as livid as the woman breathing fire before her. Or as wounded. Her expression softened. "There's obviously been some kind of misunderstanding, Ms. O'Neil—"

"You bet there has! And I intend to clear it up right now. Which office is his?"

"I'm afraid you can't see him now. He's in a strategy meeting. Wait! You can't go in there!"

Ignoring her, Philly marched past her and headed for the closed door just past the reception area. There was no name on it, but she knew the protective secretary wouldn't be very far from her boss. Grabbing the doorknob, she gave it a quick twist and pushed open the door without knocking.

"...consider another commercial. One that'll hit King where it hurts. I want him to sweat—"

Pacing while he hammered out the newest changes in the campaign with Tim, Morgan turned at the sound of the door opening and stopped dead at the sight of Philly standing only six feet away. Dressed in a big, fuzzy ivory sweater that fell to the middle of her thighs, black leggings and knee-high boots, she looked infinitely touchable, temptingly soft. Whatever he had been going to say next evaporated like raindrops on a hot rock. At his side, he felt rather than saw Tim jump to his feet to intercept her. He stopped him with nothing more than a wave of his hand without ever taking his gaze from Philly.

"I want to talk to you."

Her voice was cool, steady, impersonal. For a moment Morgan could have been forgiven for thinking she'd come to push him again on the shelter funding bill. At first glance she looked just as self-contained, just as sure of herself, as she had three days ago when she'd looked into a TV camera and defiantly challenged him in front of God and half the population of Maryland. Then he saw her eyes. Dark and stormy, the green depths churned with outrage and what looked surprisingly like hurt.

Disturbed, he took a step toward her before he realized it, then abruptly brought himself up short, frowning. He knew he could handle whatever new beef she had with him, but hurt was something else again. He knew his weaknesses, and a vulnerable female was one of them. Damn it to hell, why was she glaring at him as if he'd stabbed her in the heart?

"All right," he said quietly. "Tim, excuse us a minute, will you?" From the corner of his eye he saw his friend hesitate, obviously wanting to warn him not to do something stupid, but there was no tactful way to do so. Shooting him a speaking glance, he strode out of the office and shut the door behind him.

Silence fell like a rock between them, the tension suddenly as thick as it had been last night when he'd made the mistake of reaching for her. Fighting the need to do so again, Morgan deliberately moved behind his desk and motioned for her to take a seat.

"You want to sit down and tell me what this is all about?"

Did he really not know? she wondered incredulously. Or was this, too, another test? The restraint that had held her aloof and motionless before him snapped at the thought. Fury sparking in her eyes, she crossed his office in four long strides and tossed the box holding the bracelet onto his desk as if she could no longer even stand to touch it. "*This* is what this is all about. Recognize it?"

He only lifted a brow. "I presume it's the bracelet I sent you. What's the matter? Don't you like it?"

She stiffened as if he had slapped her. Of course she liked it! Wasn't that what he was counting on? That she'd love it on sight, thank him prettily for it, and confirm his worst suspicions about her? Dear Lord, he was smooth!

Slapping her hands flat on his desk, she leaned over until she was only inches away from him. "What I don't like, Congressman," she retorted in a voice that was too soft, too dangerous, "is being played for a fool. I know this is going to be a real blow to that rotunda-size ego of yours, but I'm not interested in you or your money or your title. I don't know how much clearer I can get. So the next time you want to *test* someone," she stressed silkily, "send a bracelet to one of those blond bimbos that hang all over you at your next fund-raiser. A woman with more bust than brains might not care that you're an arrogant, insecure, unfeeling bastard!"

Furious, she threw the words at him like darts, but it wasn't her anger that made him wince. It was her pain. She was practically shaking with it, and it was all his fault. Unable to stop himself, he started back around the desk toward her. "Philly, I never meant to hurt you—"

"Hurt me?" she repeated scathingly. "Don't flatter yourself. For someone to be able to hurt you, you've got to care about them, and I don't care two cents about you, Morgan Stewart. Do you hear me? You stay away from me, and we'll both get along just fine!"

"So what are you saying? Forget last night ever happened? Is that what you want?"

The slamming of the door behind her was his only answer.

Swearing, Morgan snatched up the box holding the bracelet and almost threw it after her. Damn it to hell, how had this happened? All he'd wanted was to prove to himself that the lady was a fortune hunter out for a free ride. Instead he'd proven nothing. Except that there was a good possibility that he was dead wrong about her. And rather than finding a reason to despise her, he realized he'd never wanted her more. Hell!

Her head held high and her steps brisk, Philly hurried through the long corridors of the Capitol without looking either left or right, afraid her tightly held control would shatter if she allowed herself to make eye contact with a single soul. Without conscious effort on her part, she skirted around anyone who got in her way, never breaking her stride, her only thought to get away before the tears clogging her throat spilled over into her eyes.

But the minute she stepped outside into the late afternoon sunshine, her vision blurred, infuriating her. The air was crisp, the sky robin's-egg blue and beautiful. She never noticed. For the first time in twenty-six years she was crying over a man, and she didn't like it one little bit.

Angrily dashing the moisture from her cheeks, she rushed pell-mell down the Capitol's steps, swearing at Morgan every step of the way. Damn him, she wouldn't let him do this to her! She wouldn't let him make her miserable when she'd been perfectly satisfied with her life until he'd come along. She had a lot of male friends, men who liked and respected her and would have been outraged by Morgan's suspicions of her. All right, so maybe none of them made her go weak at the knees and made her heart skip, but she'd never once shed a tear over any of them, either. She didn't lie awake at night thinking of them, aching for them, obsessed by a kiss that had shifted the very ground beneath her feet.

Well, it would never happen again, she promised herself, her spine ramrod-straight as she headed for her car. She wasn't one of those women who had to be burned by a fire twice before she got the message to steer clear of the flames. She had tonight and tomorrow off, and by the time she returned to work, she'd have her emotions well in hand. Come hell or high water, she'd look him right in the eye and never feel a twinge of need.

Yeah, right, Phil! a voice jeered in her head. *Try telling that to someone who believes it. Face it, the guy's under your skin, and avoiding him's not going to make you forget him.*

Maybe not, she agreed, but her pride had taken enough of a beating where Morgan Stewart was concerned. She wouldn't be one of the countless women who made fools of themselves over him, his for the asking. He'd hurt her for the last time.

Satisfied, she reached her car and unlocked it. But before she could slip into the driver's seat, a cool breeze drew her attention to a piece of paper trapped under her windshield wiper. She frowned as her stomach seemed to sink to her feet. With a murmur of disgust, she reluctantly pulled it free and looked down at a parking ticket. She had exceeded the fifteen-minute limit. Some days it just didn't pay to get out of bed.

The back door of the shelter was open, spilling light out into the night. Pulling into the parking lot, Morgan cut his engine and headlights and stared unblinkingly at the open door, his face set in grim lines. Ever since Philly had stormed out of his office two hours earlier, he'd done nothing but argue with himself. The suspicious side of his brain pointed out that a very clever fortune hunter knew better than to jump on the first carrot that was held out to her. For all he knew, she could have staged the entire bracelet-throwing incident just to put him off the scent.

An image of the hurt darkening her green eyes like a bruise flashed before his mind's eye, pricking his conscious. He swore. Even a damn fine actress would have trouble feigning that wounded expression, and after only a few days' acquaintance, even he knew Philly was no actress. Her emotions ran close to the surface, registering on her face almost as soon as they registered in her mind. If she had been pretending, he would have seen through her in a second.

So he'd insulted her, hurt her and, in general, acted like a first-class jackass. She wasn't anything like the "blond bimbos" she'd accused him of lumping her with, and that only made things worse. Every rule he had for dealing with women went right out the window when it came to her.

She claimed she wasn't interested in his money, and her actions only seemed to reinforce that. She drove a car that was as old as she was, had lived in what was little more than a tenement before it burned down and Gussy offered her the apartment over the garage, and didn't wear a lick of jewelry. She didn't seem to be looking for a husband, a high-powered job, or the rich life-style that every woman he'd ever dated had wanted to become accustomed to. Her tastes were simple enough, her wants apparently few. Yet he'd never met a more complicated female in his life. He didn't know what to expect from her and it was driving him right up the wall!

Despite that, it had still taken all of his self-control not to go after her, to apologize, to take her in his arms and kiss her until they were both senseless. Instead he'd given the bracelet to Mary to return—he never wanted to see the damn thing again—and reminded himself that Philly was a do-gooder of the worst kind, an activist, a liberal who rushed in where angels would have had second thoughts. He was and always would be conservative and cautious, a right-winger who never jumped into anything bigger than a puddle without testing the depth of the water. They might be as combustible as fireworks on the Fourth of July when they got within ten feet of each other, but they couldn't describe a sunset without disagreeing.

She was a distraction he couldn't afford, he decided as he got out of his car and approached the shelter's back door. The campaign was too close to call and King too clever to take for granted. If he was going to stay one step ahead of him between now and the first Tuesday in November, he had to put Philly out of his head and stick to business. He didn't fool himself into thinking it would be easy. He couldn't look at the woman without wanting her.

His jaw set determinedly, he walked into the shelter. But the bracing pep talk he gave himself wasn't necessary. She wasn't there.

"She decided to take a few days off," Gary explained when he saw him glance around. "Surprised the hell out of me, too. She's been working here over a month and hasn't missed a day without putting in an appearance. I kept telling her she didn't need to— that's what she had me for. What good's an assistant if you don't delegate authority and take a break once in a while?" he asked reasonably. "But you know how stubborn she is. This is her first job as a director and I think she wanted to make a good impression on the board. But falling on her face from exhaustion isn't going to win her any brownie points, either. This time off will do her good."

Morgan knew he should have been relieved. After all, wasn't that what he wanted? Time away from her so he could get his bearings? Now he could put in his four hours at the shelter in peace without being distracted by the knowledge that she was somewhere in the building. And she wouldn't be there as he left for the night, either, her memory following him home to play havoc with his concentration as he worked on the speech he would be giving in Chevy Chase on Saturday. He had her right where he wanted her—out of sight.

However, he soon learned that out of sight was anything but out of mind. If Gary wasn't talking about her, then one of the people who came in off the street was, asking about her in concern, then sighing in relief when they were told she'd only taken some time off. In self-defense, Morgan tried to lose himself in the work itself, but the shadow of her presence was everywhere. He'd hardly spent any time at all with her here, yet memories hit him in the face every time he turned around. Philly holding a baby that wasn't hers, her eyes soft with a yearning she wasn't even aware of. Philly lending a hand in the kitchen, her cheeks rosy as she bent over the stove. Philly trying her damnedest not to laugh over the fiasco with his car, her eyes bright, infectious laughter tugging at her mouth. Always Philly. This was her turf, her shelter, her world. And he couldn't shake the feeling that she wasn't here because of him.

The second night it only got worse.

It was a gloomy evening, the kind Edgar Allan Poe must have loved—cold, wet and depressing. The rain had started in the morning with a bone-chilling mist that had, over the course of the day, slowly evolved into a steady drizzle. Darkness descended without any sign of a letup in the soggy conditions, so by the time Morgan arrived at the shelter, the night wasn't fit for anything but ducks. If Gussy had seen him dodging puddles as he hurried from his car to the back door, his black umbrella dancing over his head, she would have told him it was pneumonia weather and any sane man would be at home enjoying a hot toddy. But he didn't feel sane.

A woman didn't have a right to prey on a man's mind the way Philly did his! he raged. All day long she'd popped in and out of his thoughts at random, riddling him with guilt even though he knew he'd been entitled to his suspicions of her. A half-dozen times, he'd reached for the phone, whether to apologize or to order her to leave him the hell alone he didn't know. But each time, before he could find out, he'd slam down the receiver, determined to find an excuse to avoid putting any more time in at the shelter.

Yet, here he was. And with the slightest provocation, he could have chewed nails.

Jerking open the back door, he stepped inside, shaking off water, his face hard. The minute he turned his attention to his surroundings, he knew something was wrong. Over the usual sounds of babies crying and children playing, he could hear the raised voices of a crowd of adults drowning out Gary's pleas for a little patience.

He strode to the front, his frown deepening at the sight of three families and five damp and ragged men arguing with Philly's assistant. "Problems, Gary?"

Visible relief swept over the younger man's face. "Man, am I glad to see you!" Quickly extracting himself from the horde surrounding him, he excused himself and motioned for Morgan to join him in Philly's office. Harried, he quickly shut the door and raked his fingers through his hair. "This rain has been a nightmare! People I've never even seen before have been coming in for the last two hours looking for dry ground. We're almost full up and it's not even seven o'clock!"

"How many beds do you have left?"

"Three."

Three beds for seventeen people. And it was still early. Before the evening was over, another dozen could wander in. Morgan swore under his breath. "What do you need me to do?"

For the first time in hours, Gary grinned. This wasn't Morgan's job or his cause and no one would have blamed him if he'd cut and run. The fact that he didn't earned him a new respect in Gary's eyes. Philly must have really touched a nerve when she'd challenged him.

Turning to her desk, he snatched up a list of the shelters in the area and held it out to him. "While I'm trying to keep a lid on the tempers out there," he said, nodding toward the door and the discontented crowd waiting on the other side, "you can call around and see if anyone can take our overflow. Otherwise we're going to have to send them back onto the street."

Morgan wouldn't have turned a dog out on a night like this one. Stiffly he took the list. "I'll see what I can do."

The next two hours were sobering, disturbing and frustrating. He tracked down beds like a detective combing through the city for clues, calling all the shelters on the long list until he found a place for everyone and arranging transportation for them. Then, just as he would begin to relax, satisfied that no one would spend the night out in the rain, someone else would come in, wet and cold and miserable. Once again, he would reach for the phone.

And through it all, he could almost hear Philly's voice in his ear, reproaching him for his stand against the funding bill in the face of such obvious need. When he finally went home to his whiskey by the fire tonight, would he even give a second thought to those who didn't even have a roof to get under, let alone a fire to warm themselves by?

Frustration flared in his eyes and hardened his jaw. He wasn't a monster. He hated the thought of anyone being on the streets, fighting just to survive. Especially children. Their big, solemn eyes cut at him in a way words never could. He found himself wanting to explain his position, to defend himself, to make them understand that *he* wasn't their enemy, that a vote against the funding bill wasn't a vote against them, that he could help them much more by sponsoring job programs and tax incentives that would stimulate the economy than by appropriating more money for shelters.

But they wouldn't understand any more than Philly wanted to understand. She saw only black or white and refused to even consider all the grays in between. But as an elected official, a holder of the people's trust, he had to consider all those grays, investigate the issues thoroughly and weigh both the pros and the cons. Sometimes—as in this case—there was no perfect solution. The needs of the majority had to overrule the needs of the individual, and someone had to lose out. It was unfortunate, and he hated the idea of families roaming the streets like nomads, going hungry and never having the security of knowing where they would sleep from one night to the next. But the funding bill was a stop-gap measure that he just couldn't support.

Wearily he kneaded the tense muscles at the back of his neck as the clock wound down on his shift and the shelter finally began to quiet down for the night. He'd been working too hard, sleeping too little, stretching himself too thin. He wanted to blame it on the campaign, on his schedule, on the days off he never had, but he knew there was only one reason he was pushing himself harder than usual. Philly.

His jaw locked on an oath, but there was no denying the truth. In a matter of days she'd managed to turn not only his life upside down, but his career, as well. And there didn't seem to be a damn thing he could do about it. Somehow, some way, he was going to have to find a way to deal with what she was doing to him. But not tonight.

Leaving the shelter in Gary's hands, he trudged back out into the wet darkness to his car, the only thought he'd allow himself that of the good stiff drink he was going to fix the minute he walked in his front door. It wasn't until he looked up from his brooding thoughts fifteen minutes later and hit the brakes that he realized he'd made a wrong turn.

Gussy's house sat before him in the glare of his headlights, the front windows dark and blank, shuttered for the night. A muscle flexed in his clenched jaw. For two cents he'd turn around and get the hell out of here before anyone realized he was there. But Gussy would be terribly hurt if she looked out the window and saw him leaving without even coming in to say hello.

Swearing, he circled around to the back of the house, resisting the temptation to glance at the apartment over the garage where he knew Philly was holed up against the rain, avoiding him. Instead he focused his eyes on the welcoming light shining through the kitchen windows. Gussy was probably there now, enjoying a cup of hot chocolate. Or a piece of pie, he thought with a smile. It had been too long since he'd sat at her kitchen table and enjoyed a slice of her pecan pie while she shared the latest D.C. gossip with him. Fifteen minutes, he promised himself. What could it hurt?

But when he sloshed through the rain to her back door and pushed it open after only a quick knock, Gussy was nowhere in sight. Dressed in jeans and red and white sweater, a streak of chocolate decorating one cheek, Philly stood like a stork at the butcher block, one red-socked foot planted on the floor, the other resting comfortably on the inside of her thigh, just above her knee. Icing cupcakes and laughing with a teenage boy Morgan only just then noticed sitting at the table with a book spread out before him, she looked good enough to eat herself.

And she was obviously as surprised to see him as he was to see her. She almost dropped the icing-laden knife she held before she quickly recovered, her laughter turning to cool reserve in the blink of an eye. Introducing the teenager, whose eyes had already widened in recognition, she explained, "I tutor Mark twice a week in French. Gussy's letting us use her kitchen so I can make cupcakes for the kids at the shelter while Mark studies. She's in the den."

She had given him the perfect opportunity to excuse himself, clearly indicating that there was no question in her mind who she thought he'd come to visit. Stunned, he realized she couldn't have been more wrong. And to top it all off, he knew now that he wasn't there by accident or chance. He simply hadn't been able to stay away. He was here to see Philly.

Six

She didn't want him here. She'd spent the last two days avoiding him and the last two nights cursing him, nursing a hurt that both confused and infuriated her, trying to put her feelings for him into perspective. He'd kissed her once. *Once,* for God's sake! All right, so she'd felt something—a spark, a heat, a need that made her go weak at the knees—but that still didn't change the fact that he was all wrong for her. She needed someone like her father, someone patient and kind and selfless who could work side by side with her, just as her father worked with her mother. She liked Morgan more than she wanted to, wanted him more than was wise, but she knew he would never be that kind of man. Soon he would be back on his side of the political fence, the fence that separated them. Then she would be able to stop thinking of him as anything but an adversary. Then she would stop dreaming of him.

She thought she'd had it all figured out. But the minute he walked in the door, all her fine resolves dissolved like smoke in the wind. Looking like he'd just stepped out of her best fantasy, he stood halfway across the room, his hard, angled jaw shadowed by a day's growth of beard, his dark hair wet and glistening with rain. He hadn't bothered with a jacket, and his damp sweatshirt and jeans clung to his broad shoulders and trim hips. He'd brought the wildness of the night inside with him, his mere presence charging the air with the hushed expectancy that precedes the sizzle and fire of a lightning bolt.

She felt her throat go dry, her heart thud, and paled at the strength of will it took to turn her back on him as if he'd already retreated to the den. Staring blindly at Mark, she forced a stiff smile. "Now, where were we? If I'm going to get you ready for that test tomorrow, we'd better go over your verbs. You really need some practice conjugating."

The teenager looked up at her in bewilderment. "But we already did that. Twice! Don't you remember? You said I knew them backward and forward."

Hot color singed her cheeks. "Oh! Yes, of course." Cursing herself, she could feel Morgan's eyes on her, taking in her confusion. Damn it, why didn't he go on in to Gussy and leave her alone! "Then I guess you're ready for the test," she told Mark too brightly. "Unless there's something else you'd like to go over."

She drew the question out hopefully, but Mark was already gathering up his books and slipping into his football jacket. "No, I think I got it. For now at least," he added ruefully. "Hopefully I won't blank out during the test."

"Don't run off on my account," Morgan said quietly. "Philly and I can talk later if you need more help."

He looked horrified at the thought of holding Morgan up. "Oh, no, sir! I've got it. Really. There's only so much room in my brain, and right now it's full to the brim. Thanks, anyway. I gotta go. 'Night."

He slipped out the back door quietly, leaving behind a silence that seemed to throb with every erratic beat of Philly's heart. Determinedly she kept her eyes on the cupcake she was jerkily icing, hoping Morgan would get the message that she wanted nothing to do with him. But his patience was limitless. Without saying a word, he settled himself against the counter, crossed his arms over his chest and prepared to wait her out.

Grinding her teeth in frustration, she set down the sloppily finished cupcake and wiped her sticky hands on a damp dishcloth. "If you came all the way over here just to speak to me, you wasted your time," she said flatly, meeting his watchful gaze head-on. "We did all our talking two days ago."

As if that settled the matter, she snatched up the flour canister and headed for the walk-in pantry, clearly expecting him to go. Appreciation gleamed in Morgan's eyes. She did that damn well, he thought, fighting a grin. Even in stockinged feet, with chocolate streaking her cheek, she could adopt the regality of an offended princess. If she knew how she tempted him when she did that, she wouldn't be quite so quick to lift her chin to him.

He should leave now, he told himself. While he still could. Before he made the stupid mistake of reaching for her. But he had a sinking feeling it was already too late for that. The minute he'd stepped into the kitchen, he'd known he'd never get out of there without touching her. Unable to stop himself, he followed her into the pantry.

Her back to him as she returned the flour to its place on one of the shelves that lined the small six-by-six-foot room, Philly didn't have to hear Morgan's step behind her to know when he entered the pantry. The damp, clean scent of him mingled with the aroma of sugar and spice in a devastating combination, surrounding her. He made no move to close the distance between them, but he didn't have to. Her senses were tingling as if he'd already gathered her close in his arms; her pulse was thundering as if he'd kissed her until the only breath left in her body was that she'd shared with him. She wanted to run. From herself. From him. To him. Fighting the urge, she stayed stubbornly where she was and wrapped her arms around herself, keeping her eyes trained unblinkingly on the shelf directly in front of her.

"Go away," she said tightly. *"Leave me alone."*

It was a cry from the heart, a plea for peace that struck Morgan right in the gut. Staring at her rigid back, he would have given just about anything to do as she asked. But the same unwanted attraction that was tearing at her was ripping him apart, too, and there was no walking away from it.

"Don't you think I've tried?" he demanded softly, striding closer. "I know you've been avoiding me for the last two days, and I don't blame you. I acted like an idiot!"

"Make that a spoiled, egotistical idiot, and you'll be closer to the truth."

His mustache twitched. "All right, I acted like a spoiled, egotistical idiot," he admitted. "My only excuse is that once before, I should have been suspicious of a woman, and I wasn't. I learned the hard way not to take chances."

She wanted to tell him, *Don't!* She didn't want to know about his past, didn't want to find ways to justify his actions and let go of her hurt. But she couldn't stop herself from asking, "Is that what I am to you? A chance you don't want to take?"

For a moment she thought he wasn't going to answer. He took a step toward her, then another, until his low, deep voice came from directly behind her. "I'm not a risk-taker. I like things planned right down to the last detail. Meeting a woman like you was never part of my plan, but you're a wild card I can't seem to resist." With a will of their own, his fingers reached for the dark curls that tumbled down her back. "There's something between us that keeps pulling me back to you," he said huskily. "Can't you feel it?"

"No!"

Her denial was swift and strong and blurted out far too quickly. He'd touched nothing but her hair, yet Morgan would have sworn she was already starting to tremble. "Look me in the eye and say that," he growled softly. "I dare you."

It would have served him right if she'd told him to take his dare and stuff it. But she knew she couldn't. Just because he was going back to his world in two days didn't mean that he would never step foot in hers again. Living so close to Gussy, she was bound to run into him again, and when she did, she didn't want him to think she was mooning over him like a lovesick teenager unable to let go of her first crush.

Bracing herself, she turned to face him, only to find him far closer than she'd expected. She only had to sway toward him to be in his arms. Her heart thundering, she forced herself to stand as still as a statue. "All right, if that's the way you want it," she said, then inwardly winced at the unsteadiness of her voice. How was she going to convince him of anything if she couldn't say it coolly and firmly? Struggling for a cold sophistication that was totally foreign to her nature, she bluntly lied, "The only thing pulling us back together is the funding bill. That's all. If I responded to your...kiss, that was only out of curiosity. You do have something of a reputation, Congressman."

Morgan's eyes narrowed dangerously. "So that's all you were doing when you melted in my arms? Seeing if I lived up to my reputation as a lover?"

He made her sound like a shameless jezebel, but that was just what she wanted. Wasn't it? "Yes."

"Liar."

The softly whispered taunt dropped between them like a gauntlet. She stared up at him, wondering where her outrage was, wondering why she wasn't furiously denying that she was any such thing. But the pride-saving words just wouldn't come. All she could manage was "I'm not," and even that was pitifully weak.

Without even seeming to move, he was suddenly closer. "Shall I prove it to you?" He gave her no chance to answer, no chance to push past him and escape the close intimacy of the pantry. Before she could do anything but draw in a quick, ragged breath, he captured her hand and brought it up to his mouth to press a slow, lingering kiss to the sensitive skin of her wrist. His gaze locked with hers, he stroked his tongue across her pulse.

She would have given anything to be able to stand before him unmoved by the caress. But he caught her off guard, surprising a gasp from her. Her traitorous fingers, trembling in reaction, closed into a fist, holding close the heat that radiated from her madly thumping pulse in hot waves.

Oh, God, what was she letting him do to her? Panicking, she tried to jerk free. "That's just chemistry," she cried, tugging against his hold. "It means nothing. You don't like me, you don't like what I stand for, and I'm not too crazy about you sometimes, either. So where does that leave us? With some stupid feelings that neither of us is happy about. All we have to do is ignore them, and they'll go away."

He could have told her that he did like her, that was one of the problems. He might not agree with her politics, but he had to admire her stubbornness, her tenacity, her selfless concern for others. She could create a small whirlwind when she wanted to and laugh while she did it. But she was in no mood to hear that now, and he wasn't sure he was ready to admit it.

"Some things can't be ignored," he replied, tightening his grip on her fingers as he dragged her hand down to the hard plane of his chest. Pressing her palm flat over his hammering heart, he made no attempt to hide what she did to him. "Feel that? My blood pressure skyrockets every time you get within fifty feet of me. I feel like a teenager with more hormones than he knows what to do with. And you don't want to know what the feel of you does to me. The taste..."

The low, deep rumble of his words wrapped around her, mesmerizing her, painting a picture in her mind that teased, tempted, seduced. Somewhere deep inside she knew she was in danger of being singed by the fire he was setting aflame, but even when he released his hold on her fingers at his chest, she couldn't step away from him. Her knees were too weak, her head too light from the blood that was rushing through her veins. Helpless to stop herself, she leaned toward him.

He just wanted one kiss, he told himself as his arms slipped around her. One kiss to make up for the last two nights when he'd lain awake staring at his bedroom ceiling in the dark, thinking of her until dawn, craving her in a way he'd never craved any woman. The kind of kiss he had in mind would get him through the rest of the days and nights to come while he decided exactly what he was going to do about her and the pull she had on him. That was all he needed, all he wanted.

But at the first touch of his mouth to hers, his thoughts scattered, his mind emptied. He knew Gussy was somewhere in the house; she could walk in at any minute in search of a late-night snack or a bit of friendly conversation. She would be in seventh heaven if she discovered them together like this, triumphant that her matchmaking was finally beginning to produce results. But he couldn't worry about any of that when Philly was in his arms.

He'd expected her to stiffen, to put up at least a token resistance until desire swept away her protests. But he was quickly learning that she seldom, if ever, did the expected. Instead of fighting him and herself, she yielded. Shyly. Sweetly. Completely. And just that quickly, the kiss he'd intended to take became something much, much more.

Tenderness. How did she draw it from him so effortlessly? The soft curves of her breasts met the hard plane of his chest, and suddenly he found himself swamped by a protectiveness that stunned him. He'd never met a woman more capable of taking care of herself, but all he could think of was how small she was, how breakable, how vulnerable. And on her tongue he tasted a yearning that completely undid him, calling to a dark, hidden side of his soul that he hadn't even known he had. Murmuring reassurances that he couldn't begin to ex

plain the need for, his arms urged her closer.

She'd half hoped that this kiss would be like the last, fast and furious, full of sparks and flames and needs that shattered resistance at the first touch of skin against skin. But he showed her in an instant that there was a lot to be said for taking things slow and easy. Pleasure. His fingers skimmed her spine and it spiraled through her, liquefying her bones. Like the brush of unseen wings, his hands drifted over her hips, spanning her waist, moving, always moving, until they hesitated just below her breasts.

A moan rippled through her, arching her into his palm. Care. Dear God, he took such care with her! As if she were more crushable than the petals of a rose, he stroked his thumb across the tip of her breast. Once, then twice, then once again, circling, teasing, rubbing her sweater across the silkiness of her bra as if the contrast delighted him. Whimpering, she clutched at him, her body tightening until it hummed, wanting, needing more.

Too fast, she thought hazily. This was happening too fast. Her lungs straining, her heart slamming against her ribs, she wrenched her mouth from his and buried her face against his damp sweatshirt. But that only increased her longing. With every breath she dragged in, his scent assaulted her.

"Morgan, please..."

She didn't know what she pleaded for, and she never had a chance to find out. Gussy suddenly strode into the kitchen from the den and stopped in surprise when she found the room empty. "Philly?" An instant later the sound of her footsteps crossing the floor was the only warning of her approach before she appeared in the open pantry doorway.

To her credit, she didn't bat an eye at the sight of her grandson holding her favorite renter in his arms. "Oh, I didn't know you were here, Morgan, dear. What a wonderful surprise! I didn't mean to interrupt. I just came in to see if Philly finished icing the cupcakes.''

Flushing to the roots of her hair, Philly could manage only a strangled "No" while she tried discreetly to ease out of Morgan's arms without looking like a guilty teenager.

But he was having none of it. Not even tightening his grip, he held her right where he wanted her, his gaze trained on her hot cheeks and lowered eyes. "How about some coffee, Gus? Got any made?''

"If not, it won't take me a minute to brew a pot," she replied, and turned from the doorway back into the kitchen, leaving them alone.

Nudging up Philly's chin until her eyes met his, Morgan asked quietly, "You okay?''

"Yes, of course."

But he could see that she wasn't. In her eyes was the knowledge that Gussy might have found them in a far more embarrassing position if she'd timed her arrival just five minutes later. "I'm sorry. I never meant—''

"Neither did I. Every time you touch me, I just seem to—'' Horrified at what she was admitting to, she clamped down on the revealing words and pushed against his chest, desperately needing some breathing room. This time he let her go.

Only then did her racing pulse begin to level off. Resisting the urge to hug herself, she said in a strained whisper, "I'm sure you'll agree that this can't happen again. So if you want to cut short your time at the shelter, I'll understand. It would be best for both of us if we stayed out of each other's way.''

Morgan watched her retreat to the comparative safety of the kitchen and knew he should listen to her. But she was asking the impossible. She could talk until she was blue in the face, give him a hundred reasons why they should avoid each other like the plague, but it changed nothing. Every time he touched her, he found it harder to let her go. Scowling, he followed her into the kitchen.

Gussy poured them each a cup of coffee at the kitchen table, but Philly carried hers to the work island so she could finish icing the last few cupcakes for the shelter. Studiously keeping her eyes on her task, she didn't even look up as Gussy told Morgan, "I'm so glad you dropped by, dear. I've been meaning to call you about the dance Saturday. You're going, of course."

Morgan almost groaned at the reminder. The annual Republican dinner and dance was one of those stiff, formal, fund-raising affairs where people bussed cheeks without touching, laughed without really smiling and gossiped while they danced. The food was always lukewarm, the speeches stilted, the glad-handing endless. But every mover and shaker in Washington would be there, and there was no avoiding it.

"Yes, I'll be there," he said with a grimace as he pulled out a chair at the table. "It's too important to miss."

Gussy beamed at him, pleased. "Good. So will Philly. You can go together."

"What!" Alarmed, Philly dropped the cupcake she was holding icing-side down, but it was Gussy she

stared at in horror. "Oh, no! I couldn't possibly—"
Her hands as agitated as her voice, she grabbed a
dishcloth to wipe up her mess but ended up twisting it
in knots instead. "It's a fund-raiser, isn't it? My God,
the tickets must be a thousand dollars a plate—"

"Oh, don't worry about that," Gussy said easily.
"I've already taken care of that. Dolores St. John isn't
going to be able to make it and gave me her ticket. I
want you to use it."

"But—"

"Every conservative Republican who ever made
your life miserable will be there," she continued,
holding out a carrot she knew Philly wouldn't be able
to refuse. "Including members of the Appropriation
Committee. This would be a good time for you to talk
to them one on one and try to sway them over to your
side of the funding bill. How can you even consider
not going?"

Philly hesitated, torn. It wasn't the party she was
objecting to. It was the idea of going with Morgan on
what was almost a real date. Of being with him in his
world instead of hers, watching him in his element,
surrounded by men and women whose backgrounds
were as different from hers as Georgetown was from
the reservation in Arizona where she'd spent her high
school years. Women would flock to him, just as they
always did, and she'd put a definite cramp in his style.
She wouldn't be able to look him in the eye without
feeling like Gussy had thrust her on him. And so far,
he hadn't said a single word to make her think otherwise.

"I'm sure Morgan already has a date."

He could have taken the easy way out and lied, and neither she nor Gussy would have pushed the issue. Just days ago, he would have jumped at the chance. But nothing was as it had been days ago. "No, I don't," he replied. "I'll pick you up at seven."

She wanted to argue, to point out to him that the last thing he wanted to do was encourage Gussy in her matchmaking. But she couldn't. She was trapped and they both knew it. Twisting the dishcloth in her hands into a tight double knot, she nodded mutely, wondering all the while what kind of madness she had set herself up for.

Long before the night of the dance arrived, she knew she'd made a mistake. They managed to be excessively civil to each other as Morgan finished the last of his volunteer work at the shelter, but whenever their eyes chanced to meet, they were both reminded of the heated encounter in Gussy's pantry. Her defenses already weakened, Philly had to remind herself that he was still stubbornly opposed to the funding bill. Yet every time she looked up, he was playing with the children, stepping in to help wherever he was needed without having to be asked and having long, quiet discussions with the nightly residents about their hopes and dreams and needs. She couldn't doubt his sincerity, his caring, his concern. Confused, her emotions in a turmoil, she knew suddenly she was seeing the real Morgan Stewart, a man she found it all too easy to like. And all too hard to resist.

She should have told him then that it would be better if he found someone else to go with him to the dance. After all, it wasn't as if he were hard up for a date. Washington was full of women who would be only too happy to drop at his feet if he'd just offer them a smile. But she wasn't one of them. She couldn't be. She was too vulnerable where he was concerned, too attracted to him in spite of the fact that they couldn't discuss the weather without arguing about the color of the sky.

Yet, when it came down to actually picking up the phone and canceling, she couldn't make herself do it. She couldn't deny herself one last evening with him. It wasn't as if they were going out on a *real* date, she reasoned. He was just giving her a ride to the dance. Once they arrived, he would be caught up in his crowd of supporters and she had her own work to do. She'd see him in passing; he'd bring her home afterward, then drive right out of her life. End of story.

Convinced she had her foolish heart well in hand by the time the night of the dance arrived, she opened her front door to him promptly at seven and realized that she'd made one grave miscalculation. This might not be a real date, but Morgan was dressed in a tux, his hair slightly tousled from the wind, and he looked like he'd just stepped out of a fairy tale. His eyes, fierce as a hawk's, met hers, and suddenly she felt like Cinderella being picked up for the ball. How was she ever going to get him out of her dreams after this?

Morgan could only stare at her, the smooth, easy greeting he'd intended to give her turning to dust on his tongue. Lord, she was beautiful! Her hair was caught up in a loose, sexy chignon that made a man wonder how many pins he would have to remove before he could send the dark curls tumbling down her back, but it was her dress that drove the breath from his lungs. Her shoulders were left temptingly bare by a gold sequined strapless top that clung sweetly to the curves of her breasts. Dropping his gaze to the multi-colored scarf that cinched her small waist, his eyes took a slow tour of the full, gauzy black skirt that fell all the way to her gold-sandaled feet. She was exqui-site, dainty, her only jewelry the gold hoops at her ears and the slim gold chain at her wrist. Just looking at her made him ache.

"You look wonderful."

The compliment came out in a low, rough growl that made her toes curl in response. If he'd touched her then, she'd have been tempted to suggest that they forget the party and forget their differences, forget that this was the one and only night they would prob-ably ever go out together. They could spend the eve-ning together in her apartment. Alone.

That was when she knew she would be in trouble if she didn't find a way to defuse the tension between them. *Now.*

"Thank you," she said with a coolness she was far from feeling. "But it's just bait." At the surprised lift of his brow, she explained, "I'm only going with you tonight because Gussy was right. This will be the per-fect opportunity to press for more support for the funding bill. So I dressed the part. Sometimes you have to wrap something in pretty paper before you can get people's attention." Hurriedly grabbing up her coat, she shrugged into it before he could help her. "Shall we go?"

The evening went downhill from there.

She should have been happy with the results of her handiwork. By the time they settled in his car for the drive to the hotel where the party was being held, the hunger she'd seen in Morgan's eyes when she'd first opened her door to him was gone, replaced by a scowl that showed every sign of becoming permanent. Outside the night air was cool, but it was nothing compared to the chill inside the car. For the next twenty minutes they didn't exchange a half-dozen words.

Things only got worse when they reached the party. She'd always been aware of the differences in their worlds, but never more so than when she stepped into a ballroom full of some of the most famous people in the country. Politicians, actors, rock stars and C.E.O.'s—they glittered like gold right before her eyes. There was old money, new money and all the levels of class in between. Morgan greeted a world-famous evangelist like an old friend, then laughed as a professional golfer slapped him on the back and teased him about his swing. She wasn't starstruck, but she was impressed. He moved through the country's biggest names as if he were greeting family at a backyard barbecue.

And at every turn, there were women, some shy, some bold, some old, some obviously just the right age for him, all eager for his attention. All more at ease with him than she ever was. She told herself not to watch, but even when she turned away in search of a familiar political face, she knew where he was at every moment.

Seven

He couldn't keep his eyes off her.

From the far corner of the ballroom, Morgan found himself snared by one of his grandfather's old friends into a heated discussion on the capital gains tax, but it was Philly who captured his attention and drew his eyes across the room in spite of his best efforts to ignore her. Without ever seeming to look in her direction, he was aware of every man she talked to, every man she laughed with, every partner who held her close and waltzed her through the swirling couples on the dance floor. Disgusted with himself, he deliberately turned his back on her and tried to convince himself he didn't care who she danced with, who she flirted with, who she left with. She was a free agent, only there to garner support for her cause. He didn't care what she did.

But even while he reassured friends and constituents that he was looking out for their interests, he couldn't shake the image of Philly in the arms of his colleagues, chatting with them as if they were long-lost buddies, showing them a gracious side of herself she rarely showed him. And, damn it, he resented it!

A voice in his head snorted at that. *Why don't you quit beating around the bush and admit what's really bothering you? For the first time in your life, you're jealous as hell and you don't like it.*

Stunned, he flatly refused to consider such a ridiculous possibility. But every time another man smiled at her, touched her, pulled her into his arms for a dance, his expression grew grimmer. Struck with a primitive need to pull her away from anyone who made the mistake of looking at her twice, he wanted nothing more than to cross over to her and claim her as his own. Dear God, what had she done to him?

He grabbed a drink from a passing waiter and downed it in a single gulp, hoping it would clear his head. But alcohol wasn't the answer. Steering clear of Philadelphia O'Neil was. Somehow he had to find a way to stay away from her before he did something stupid.

He might have made it through the evening without acting like a Neanderthal if she just hadn't danced with Jake Donaldson. Until then, he'd managed to keep a tight rein on the emotions clawing at him by steadfastly keeping a crowd between them. Pleased with his self-control, he'd turned from a conversation about Hollis King's latest exploits and stopped dead in his tracks at the sight of Philly in the arms of the recently divorced congressman from Texas.

Long before Donaldson's wife had kicked him out of their Arlington home, the man had had a reputation for blatantly chasing anything in skirts. Philly had to know that he had more moves than an octopus, yet there she was dancing with him, smiling at him as if he were the greatest thing since sliced bread.

Morgan gritted his teeth on an oath. If she wanted to play with fire, it was none of his business. She was a big girl; she could certainly take care of herself. Then Donaldson's hand slid down her back past her waist, urging her closer, and Morgan just lost it.

He never remembered making his way through the crush of people who blocked his path. A red haze of anger clouding his vision, he headed straight for Philly, the hard set of his angled jaw daring anyone to get in his way. No one did.

The hand he laid on Donaldson's shoulder was no soft tap, but Morgan silently congratulated himself on his self-restraint. What he really wanted to do was flatten the man with one well-aimed blow to his weak chin. "I believe this is my dance," he said coldly. "Excuse us, Donaldson."

Scowling, the older man shook off his hand as if Morgan were a pesky fly. "Forget it, Stewart. Go find your own partner. This one's mine."

His careless claim set fire to Morgan's temper quicker than a lit match. His blue eyes darkening like an approaching storm, he ignored the dancers whirling and bobbing around them and growled, "You're the loser here, Donaldson. The lady came with me. I suggest you let her go.''

Or else.

The threat was never spoken, but it hung in the air nonetheless. Alarmed, Philly could just see the headlines now. ''Congressmen Fight For Dance.'' Tugging her hand free of Jake's, she reached for Morgan. ''Wait. I—''

But he was in no mood to wait for anything. His fingers closed over hers, and in the next instant she was pulled out of Donaldson's arms and into his own. Before she could do anything more than gasp, he smoothly swung her away from the glowering Texan and into the crowd of waltzing couples, who had been watching the tense scene with barely concealed curiosity.

Philly never noticed the watchful eyes that followed their progress across the dance floor, never heard the speculative whispers that spread like wildfire around them. Her heart thundering wildly in her ears, all her attention was focused on the feel of Morgan's arms tightening around her, molding her to him without ever losing step to the music. Moments ago Donaldson had tried to do the same thing and only managed to make her skin crawl. She'd tried discreetly to put some distance between them, without much success, and had been on the verge of taking more drastic measures when Morgan had swooped down to her rescue.

Dragging in a shaky breath, she tipped her head back and tried to laugh off the near disaster. ''I've never been so glad to see anyone in my life! I was afraid I was going to have to slap his face, which was no more than he deserved, but I wasn't looking forward to it. With all the press here, I probably would have ended up on the front page of tomorrow's *Post*."

The smile she expected from him never materialized. Glaring down at her with glacial eyes, he said harshly, "What did you expect? You try to influence votes by flirting with a man like Donaldson, he's going to expect you to come across. You shouldn't play if you don't know the rules of the game."

Shocked, she missed a step and would have tripped over his feet if he hadn't caught her. "I didn't—I never—"

"The hell you didn't." His hands tightened on her, molding her to him even when he knew he should be pushing her away. She was too close, the feel of her in his arms too perfect, and his control was nearly shot to hell. Unable to stop himself, he raked his gaze down over the strapless spangled top that had drawn every male eye in the room.

"You said yourself that sometimes you have to wrap a problem up in pretty paper to get anyone to notice it," he said harshly, steering her toward the wall of French doors that opened onto the dark, shadowed balcony. "Well, sweetheart, you're wrapped real pretty tonight. If you want to seduce someone into changing their vote, why don't you try me? I'm ready, willing and just as available as Donaldson."

"Damn it, Morgan, I told you—" Her protest broke off abruptly as she suddenly realized that he was pulling her tighter against him with one hand while the other reached for the handle to the door leading to the balcony. She stiffened. "What are you doing? We can't go out there. I don't have my coat. It's cold—"

"Don't worry," he promised huskily. "I'll keep you warm."

"No!"

But it was already too late. In the next instant he had backed her out onto the empty balcony and shut the door behind them, shutting out the crowd, the music, the world. In the distance the Capitol and the Washington Monument were brightly lit beacons in the night, but their light couldn't penetrate the cold, dark shadows that engulfed the balcony.

Shivering against the icy wind that kissed her bare shoulders, Philly struggled to hang on to reason when it suddenly didn't seem like a night meant for logic at all. "Morgan, I don't know what you're trying to prove, but this is—"

Her words ended in a muffled gasp of surprise as he snatched her up against his chest and crushed his mouth to hers. Stunned, her hands flew up to his chest, whether to clutch at him or push him away she couldn't say because suddenly she couldn't think, couldn't do anything but feel.

Anger. For the first time she realized just how furiously angry he was. His body was tight with it, his hands rough with frustration as they swept over her, hauling her closer, then closer still, as if he would draw her right inside him if only he could get past the barrier of their clothes. Civilization was just beyond the French doors, but it might have been light-years away for all the notice he gave it. There in the shadows, where no one could see, he showed her a side of himself few people ever saw. Morgan Stewart, pushed to the limit, desperate with need, his usual iron control balanced on a razor-sharp edge.

Dazed, her breath coming out in short gulps, her head reeling, Philly felt as if she'd just stepped into a blazing inferno. Flames licked at her, consuming her, melting her own anger, leaving her nothing to cling to, nothing to protect her foolish heart with. Except hurt.

If you want to seduce someone into changing their vote, why don't you try me? I'm ready, willing and just as available as Donaldson.

Even as her tongue responded to the seducing dance of his, his cutting words flayed her like a cracking whip, drawing blood. A sob rose in her throat. He despised her, she thought, whimpering. He kissed her as if he couldn't get enough of her, yet he actually thought she was capable of seducing a man to win support for her cause. She should have hated him for that; she should have pushed out of his arms and told him what she thought of him. It was no more than he deserved. But still she wanted him. No man had ever hurt her before so quickly, so easily, so deeply, and yet still made her ache.

Suddenly she knew she couldn't take any more. Of his anger or his passion. She wanted to cry, to rail at him, to give in to the absurd yearning to melt against him and let him mend the heart he had just bruised without a qualm. Instead she wrenched her mouth free and pushed out of his arms before he could guess her intentions.

His heart slamming against his ribs, urgency throbbing deep in his gut, Morgan murmured a protest and instinctively reached for her, only to freeze at the sight of the hurt clouding her green eyes, silently reproaching him. Something about the way she hugged herself, as if she were protecting herself from him instead of the cold, struck him right in the heart. His blood cooled, clearing his head. Damn his temper, what had he said to her? What had he accused her of? "Philly, I—"

"No, don't!" she choked out. "I think you've said enough...done enough. I never should have come with you tonight, but I let Gussy talk me into it because I wanted to be with you. My mistake."

"If you'll just let me explain—"

But there was nothing he could say that she wanted to hear. Not now, when her eyes were brimming and she was in danger of making a fool of herself in front of half of Washington. Blinking rapidly, she stepped past him and jerked open the French door, whispering only a husky "Good night" before quickly losing herself in the crowd in the ballroom.

There was no question of staying after that. Without checking her pace, she found her way to the coatroom and requested her coat from the attendant, excusing the stupid tears that spilled over her lashes by claiming she had something in her eye. Moments later, feeling as if she were running from the devil himself, she hurried out the front entrance of the hotel and looked wildly around for a cab. It would cost her the earth, but she was in no mood to search out the nearest bus line. She just wanted to get home as quickly as possible and forget tonight had ever happened.

Spying a taxi, she brushed at her wet cheeks and hailed it with a wave of her hand. Seconds later it jerked to a stop in front of her as the driver quickly rolled down his window. "Where to, lady?"

"Bethesda," she said with a sigh of relief as she reached for the handle to the back door. "I live on—"

"I'll see the lady home," Morgan said quietly from behind her, catching her elbow with one hand while he slipped the driver a ten with the other. "She's with me."

Startled, Philly saw him take in her still-damp cheeks in one quick, all-consuming glance and wanted to die of mortification. Suddenly tired of fighting him and herself, she drew herself up with a solemn dignity, pulled free of his touch, and said, "That's not necessary. I'm perfectly capable of finding my way home by myself."

His hand fell to his side, but his blue eyes held a steely glint that warned her this was something he wasn't going to budge on. "I know you'd like me to take a long walk off a short pier right about now, but when I pick a woman up, I take her home. I'm sorry, sweetheart, but you're not leaving here without me."

"Lady, do you want a cab or not? I ain't got all night!"

At the cabbie's plaintive cry, Morgan arched a mocking brow. "Yeah, lady, you want a cab or not? What's it going to be?"

If she insisted on taking the taxi, she didn't doubt for a minute that he'd ride all the way out to Gussy's with her, then turn around and come right back for his car. She'd end up feeling like an idiot and give herself one more reason to regret this night. Sighing in defeat, she gave in. "I'm sorry," she told the cabbie, "it seems I already have a ride."

She promised herself she wouldn't say a word to him all the way home. But once they were enclosed together in the car, the silence broken only by the steady hum of the heater and the soft purr of the engine, the quiet grated on her nerves like the screech of a siren that wailed on and on. She caught herself twisting her hands in her lap and chewing her bottom lip and had to force herself to sit still. But that only drew her attention to Morgan's hand on the stick shift near her knee, smoothly down-shifting while his left thigh flexed as he let out the clutch. She found herself watching him, remembering the desperate hunger of his kiss on that balcony. Her heart started to race, and when he flicked a glance at her as they finally turned onto Gussy's property, she could have sworn he heard it.

"You don't have to drive around to the back," she said quickly as he approached the fork in the circular drive that branched off to the side of the house and curved around to the garage at the rear. "Just let me out here. I'll walk the rest of the way."

"When you can ride in a warm car?" he scoffed, heading for the back. "Don't be ridiculous. It won't take a minute."

Seconds later he braked to a stop in front of the stairs that led to the garage apartment and cut the engine. Desperate to avoid an awkward good-bye scene, Philly reached for the door handle.

"We need to talk."

She told herself to ignore the quiet timbre of his words and end what was between them here and now. He didn't trust her and never would, and a quick, clean break would be best for both of them. All she had to do was wish him a nice life and get out of the car. But her fingers flatly refused to open the door.

Turning her head sharply away, she stared blindly out the window. "We have nothing to talk about. This is it. The end of the line. After tonight, we'll never see each other again. What else is there to say?"

"How about I'm sorry?" he said gruffly, wishing she would turn around and face him, but making no move to touch her. "I know I acted like a heel out there on that balcony, and you have every right to hate my guts. My only excuse is that I couldn't stand the thought of another man's hands on you. Especially a letch like Donaldson."

Philly stiffened, unable to believe what she was hearing. She'd been so sure he despised her, so sure that he really believed all those accusations he'd thrown at her. Glancing back over her shoulder, her eyes searched his shadowed face in the darkness. "Are you saying you were jealous?"

His mouth curled in a mocking half smile at her incredulous tone. "Yeah, it was something of a surprise to me, too. I guess I didn't handle it too well, did I? If it's any consolation to you, you're the only woman who has ever made me act like a caveman. All I could think about was getting you in the dark somewhere . . . touching you . . . kissing you."

His voice thickened, his blood heated. Unable to stop himself, he leaned across the console and lifted his hand to her cheek and slowly traced the enticing curve of it. Silk. Her skin was like watered silk, soft and smooth and oh, so responsive to his touch. "I'm sorry if I hurt you," he whispered in the heated silence. Sliding his fingers to the sassy jut of her chin, he tilted her head up just enough so he could see into the dark, bottomless depths of her bewitching eyes. "Can you ever forgive me?"

Philly stared up at him and knew she was teetering on the edge of falling into his arms and into something that she would never find her way out of. Unaware that her fingers had wrapped around his wrist to keep his hand at her chin, she watched, fascinated, as emotions passed through his blue eyes like clouds racing before a storm. Desire so warm it scorched her right down to her toes. Yearning so dark that it tugged at her like the deep shadows of a summer night. Turmoil so turbulent that it drove every thought from her head but that of soothing him. The need to bolt for safety forgotten, the fingers holding his wrist sought the drumming of his pulse and stroked lightly, again and again, whispering across his skin. "We've both been under a lot of strain and said things we didn't mean," she said softly. "Let's just forget it."

He should have released her right then, gotten out of the car and walked her to her door in the head-clearing coldness of the night. But the slow, mesmerizing rhythm of her touch sent his blood pressure shooting through the roof, and he couldn't bring himself to let her go, couldn't bring himself to resist the sweet, intoxicating lure of her.

Releasing her chin abruptly, he ran his hands over the delicate bones of her wrists and up her arms, warming himself with her, absorbing her fire. But it wasn't enough. Murmuring her name, he buried his face at her throat and filled his senses with her clean, fresh scent. "God, honey, I need you," he groaned. "Let me touch you...hold you."

The BMW wasn't made for intimate contact. The console dug into her hip, the stick shift into her thigh, and Morgan couldn't move without banging his elbow against the steering wheel. Just touching was awkward; anything more would have been too uncomfortable to sustain any kind of deeper passion. But the minute he pressed her close and planted tiny, biting kisses across her neck to the hollow behind her ear, she wouldn't have noticed if they were in a sardine can. She clung to him, sinking fast into a whirlwind of swirling colors that stole her breath. Her breath shuddering through her lungs, her head fell back helplessly against his shoulder at the feel of his fingers at her throat, fumbling with the buttons of her coat, tearing at them. Then her shoulders were bare and her arms free and his mouth was rushing over her, devouring.

"Morgan..."

She whispered his name in a voice that was so low and sultry with need she hardly recognized it. Seeming to know where she ached to be touched even before she did, he yanked down the zipper to her gold spangled top and bared her breasts to his eyes, to his gently kneading hands, to the hot stab of his tongue. With a startled cry, she arched against him, blindly offering herself, her fingers tunneling through his dark hair to hold him close as pleasure shot through her like a heat-seeking missile.

Madness. He'd never known a woman who could push him this close to it so easily, so effortlessly. After the way he'd treated her earlier, she should have hauled off and hit him the minute he'd touched her. Instead she was yielding, giving of herself so completely she was making him forget his own name. God, how he wanted her! Here, now, this very instant, naked and bare underneath him, surrounding him, driving him out of his mind. He had her halfway there already. All he had to do was get her out of that skirt, strip her of her panty hose— Suddenly realizing just how close he was to losing control, he brought his hot, wild thoughts to a bone-jarring halt. What the hell was he doing? he thought, clamping his teeth on a savage curse. He'd never, ever, taken a women in his car. Never, ever been so lost to passion that he'd thought of assuaging the need tearing at him before he thought of his partner's comfort first.

With fingers that were anything but steady, he dragged her hands from his hair and pulled them around behind his waist in a hug that forced her breasts against his chest and her face against his throat. But in the instant before her face was hidden to him, he caught the sheen of dazed, bewildered passion in her eyes. A muscle ticked along his jaw. Holding her tight, he ignored the fires raging in his body and growled, "Honey, we need to talk about the effect we have on each other."

Throbbing, her heart laboring like a runaway horse, Philly couldn't seem to manage the mouth-tongue coordination needed to speak. She swallowed, her fingers curling into Morgan's back, the only handhold she could find at the moment. "Now?"

"Right now," he agreed, tightening his arms around her. "In case you hadn't noticed, we go up in flames every time we get within touching distance."

She started to nod, then obviously thought better of rubbing her head against him. Her arms still holding on to him like a lifeline, she went perfectly still. "I noticed."

"You may have also noticed that each time I hold you, I find it harder and harder to let you go. We both know if we keep this up, there'll come a time when I may not be able to. No," he corrected grimly, "let me rephrase that. I want you too badly to keep letting you go. One of these days I won't be able to. Just now I came damn close to taking you right here in the car."

And she would have let him.

Suddenly realizing just what that implied, Philly stiffened, stunned. She could never have even considered giving herself to him unless she was dangerously close to loving him. The knowledge hit her like a bucket of ice water, rocking her back on her heels. No! she almost cried out. She couldn't be on the verge of falling in love with a man she could never share a future with. She couldn't be that foolish!

Suddenly desperate to be alone, to think, she pushed out of his arms, heat firing her cheeks as she jerked up her top with shaking fingers. "I—I h-have to go...in." Fumbling behind her for the zipper, she swore in mounting agitation when she couldn't find the tab.

Baffled by her abrupt change in mood, Morgan moved to help her. "Honey, what is it? What's wrong? Here, let me help—"

"No!" Her cry was short, sharp, frantic. Evading his hands, she abandoned her sagging top and snatched up her coat. In the span of two heartbeats, she jerked it on and whipped it shut over her bare breasts. Even then, she couldn't look at him. The tears were stinging her eyes and burning her throat, and it would only take one touch, one look from him to shatter her. Blindly, she reached for the door handle.

"Sweetheart, wait!"

He reached for her, but he was too late. Before he could touch her, she was gone, slamming the door behind her.

Eight

"*Once again, my dear readers, one of the Hill's most eligible bachelors is the talk of the town. With a royal challenger hot on his tail for his congressional seat and a lovely social worker intent on making his life miserable for refusing to support her cause, the poor boy hasn't had a thing to smile about for weeks. The challenger is still waiting in the wings to steal his thunder, but who do you think we spied dancing in the moonlight and kissing in the dark during last night's Republican powwow? You guessed it! The blue-eyed boy wonder and his petite nemesis. One can only wonder if she's the same lady he bought a gorgeous antique*

bracelet for just last week. What do you say,
Congressman? Have you and the lady de-
cided to make love instead of war? Or has
she finally found a way to convince you to
support her cause?"

Gussy finished reading the gossip column aloud and
threw the morning paper down on Philly's small
kitchen table with a snort of disgust. "Garbage," she
said contemptuously, her blue eyes flashing with outrage. "Who does Sarah Connors think she's fooling
with her silly innuendos? *Royal challenger,*" she
mimicked. "Why didn't she just print King's name
and be done with it? Everyone knows who she's talking about."

Stricken, Philly sank down onto a chair across the
table from Gussy, her face as pale as ivory, her hair
tousled, her eyes bruised from the long sleepless hours
she'd lain in bed fighting feelings that could only lead
to disaster. Sometime around dawn, she'd finally accepted the fact that the best thing she could do for
both of them was get out of Morgan's life before one
of them got hurt. Then Gussy had banged on her door
at seven-thirty, the newspaper clutched in her hand
and murder in her eyes, and she'd known she'd waited
too long.

Working up a full head of steam, the older woman
paced restlessly. "How dare she imply that you would
use sex to try to change Morgan's mind about his stand
on the funding bill," she fumed. "That's outrageous!
I've half a mind to call Joseph Tinkerton himself and

tell him what I think of the yellow journalism he's publishing down there at that damn paper of his!''

She was halfway to the phone when Philly stopped her. "Gussy, don't! Please..."

"These are nothing but unsubstantiated lies designed to stir up trouble. We may not be able to do anything about it, but I can give Tinkerton an earful, I promise you that!"

Suddenly chilled, Philly wrapped her battered yellow chenille robe tighter around her, color singeing her pale cheeks. "But I did kiss him," she admitted huskily. "More than once."

"So?" Gussy retorted, not batting an eye. "Since when is it a crime for a man and a woman to be attracted to each other? To share a kiss in the dark? You're both single, both free to do whatever you want without having to answer to anyone. Sarah Connors," she continued, jabbing at the paper, "had no right to spy on a private moment between you, then twist it with innuendos and print it in the paper for all the world to speculate about."

Snatching up the paper, she threw it in the trash as if that would alleviate the problem. But her eyes were worried when she turned back to Philly. "This isn't the kind of publicity Morgan needs this close to the election. A lot of people will dismiss it as nothing but gossip, but there are always those who haven't made up their mind yet, who are looking for a reason not to vote for the incumbent. This may be it."

Guilt washed over Philly, squeezing her heart. She never should have gone with him last night, never should have let herself get personally involved with him, never should have publicly challenged him in the first place. She'd only been thinking of herself and what she wanted, what was important to her and the people in her life, and hadn't given a thought to what she might be costing him. If he lost the election because of her, she'd never be able to forgive herself.

Too agitated to sit still, she moved to the stove to put on a pot of coffee. Her back to Gussy, she said quietly, "I know this is too little, too late, but I decided last night that I'm not going to see him again."

"But—"

"Face it, Gus, it's just not going to work," she said quickly, turning to face her. "We're too different. Morgan has his life all planned out, all the i's dotted and the t's crossed. A man in his position, with his ambitions, has to know where he's going and not let anything get in the way. You know me, I love change! I can get sidetracked on the way to the grocery store. Even if we agreed on everything else in our lives—and that would take a miracle—we'd still drive each other nuts within a matter of weeks." She smiled wistfully, regretfully. "Some things just aren't meant to be."

She stood there with her chin up, trying desperately to be practical, her arguments all lined up like ducks in a row. But she had to bite her bottom lip to keep it from quivering, and her eyes had a lost look that almost broke Gussy's heart. She wanted to go to her then, to wrap her arms around her and assure her that she was worrying about nothing. If they loved each other enough, and she suspected they did, anything was possible.

But that was something Philly and Morgan had to find out for themselves. She'd done everything she could to get them together. The rest was up to them. "Are you sure this is what you want?"

Philly would have laughed at that if she hadn't been so afraid it would come out as a sob. She would not cry! "No, it isn't what I want. But it's what I can live with. What I *have* to live with," she stressed sadly. "Because hoping for anything more just hurts too much."

Tim prowled the confines of Morgan's office like a defendant waiting for the jury to come back with a verdict, the society page crushed in his hand. Seated stiffly at his desk, his face stony, Morgan didn't need to take a second look at the gossip column to know what it said. He'd read it over coffee, then been hit with it again by Tim the minute he stepped into his office. Every word was indelibly etched in his brain.

Rage burning in his gut, Morgan thought of Philly reading it and wanted to throw something. This wasn't the first time his name had been linked with a woman's in the paper. But always before he hadn't given it a thought because the women he'd dated had enjoyed the publicity, in some cases even sought it out. Philly, however, was different. She would welcome publicity for the shelter, for the homeless, but never for herself. What they shared in the dark wasn't for publication, and he could just imagine her embarrassment when she read the columnist's speculation about them.

He needed to call her, he thought grimly, warn her, tell her to ignore it because it was just trash. But he knew she wouldn't. She'd take it straight to heart. Damn, he wanted to see her, to hold her....

"Maybe we're overreacting here," Tim said hopefully, breaking into his musings. "Sarah Connors is known for her innuendos and half-truths. She could find something to gossip about at a kid's birthday party. No one takes her seriously."

Morgan only lifted a brow. They both knew that even a blatant lie could hurt in an election year.

Swearing, Tim tugged at the tie that nearly choked him and knew he had no choice but to agree. "You're right. People believe what they want to believe. It doesn't matter if it's the truth or not. Hell, most times they'd rather believe a lie. It's usually a heck of a lot more interesting."

Scowling, he resumed wearing out the carpet. "Then we've got to come up with a way to nip the gossip in the bud before King has a field day with it," he said, tearing at his tie. "A denial wouldn't do anything but spark the interest of people who haven't seen the column, so your best bet is to get out of town for a while. I suggest you start stumping Maryland now instead of waiting as planned for the October recess on the nineteenth. Talk'll die down soon enough if you're at one end of the state and Ms. O'Neil's at the other."

Morgan only grunted, not surprised by the suggestion. The only thing that mattered to Tim was the election. He would do anything within the law, advise any course of action that would lead to a victory on the first Tuesday in November. He wouldn't think twice about leaving Philly to deal with the local press if he thought it would help Morgan in the polls.

"I'm not going to let Philly take the heat from this alone," Morgan warned him coldly.

"So what are you going to do?" he countered. "Come riding to her rescue like a knight on a white charger? King'll just love that!"

"Damn it, I don't give a flying leap about King!" Wanting to break something, he pushed back from his desk and surged to his feet. "This has nothing to do with that worm! Or the election. What happened between Philly and me last night is no one's business but ours."

Tim would have liked to agree with him, but he got paid to play devil's advocate, not be a yes-man. "If you were a bank officer or a stockbroker or some Joe Blow on the street, I'd say you had a legitimate beef. But you're not. You're an elected official. A *single* elected official," he stressed. "That makes you vulnerable to this type of attack."

Morgan stiffened. "Don't start, Tim. I don't want to hear it."

But the other man wasn't so easily discouraged from his favorite topic. "Well, it's true. If you were married to the right kind of woman, your private life would be above reproach. Think about it," he said eagerly. "You'd have a built-in hostess, a real home with kids and dogs and a station wagon. You'd be so damn boring the gossips would have to find someone else to talk about, and opponents like King couldn't make your love life one of the issues of the campaign. You'd have it made in the shade."

Morgan only glared at him. When Tim talked about the "right kind of woman," he wasn't talking about a wife, but an asset. A rich, beautiful, well-educated, politically connected female who knew how to dress like a model, act like a princess and wanted nothing more in life than to stand in his shadow and further his career. She sounded like a dead bore.

The woman who haunted his every waking moment would never stand in any man's shadow. Her long dark hair was too wild to tamely accept confinement for long and she didn't give a hang about how much money she had in her checking account. More often than not, her impish face was free of makeup, her tempting mouth bare of lipstick. She would never be as tall as a model, as well-behaved as a princess, but she could drive him right out of his mind with wanting.

"Forget it," he retorted. "You want that kind of wife, find yourself one. The only woman I'm interested in right now is Philadelphia O'Neil."

Tim swore softly. "I was afraid of that. Damn it to hell, Morgan, you're playing with fire here! If you want to beat King, I'm warning you to stay away from that woman. At least until after the election. She's publicly challenged you, publicly criticized you. You keep seeing her and the voters are going to wonder if your hormones have scrambled your brains."

Morgan almost told him to go to the devil. No one told him who he could or couldn't see. But he couldn't take a chance on losing the election, either. Politics was in his blood. Following in his grandfather's footsteps, working in the very chamber where the old man had left his mark on history, helping people he didn't even know, was the only thing he'd ever wanted to do. He had to win!

Which meant he had to follow Tim's advice, he reluctantly acknowledged. He hadn't hired him as his campaign manager because he was his friend, but because he had a nose like a bloodhound and a mind like a steel trap. He knew how the constituents thought, voted, prayed, and what they expected from their elected representatives. If he said just being in the same city with Philly could hurt him now, when he needed to go into November with strong numbers in the polls, you could damn well bet he knew what he was talking about.

"All right," he sighed heavily. "I'll think about pushing up my schedule. Okay? But even if I do decide to do it, I can't completely abandon my committee work. I'll still have to make occasional trips back to D.C."

His words carried the hint of a warning, but Tim only nodded. They both knew any returns to the capitol before the eve of the election would be quick, harried and all business. There would be no time for any outside distractions, and no time for Philly before he had to leave again.

At two in the afternoon, the shelter was quiet and nearly empty, the only sound the soft hum of the radio coming from the kitchen, where Gary was already supervising the preparations for the spaghetti and meatballs dinner the shelter served every Thursday night. Hunched over her desk in her office, Philly told herself it was the perfect time to catch up on her paperwork. She had grant applications to fill out, her monthly report to write for the director's meeting next week, supplies to inventory and order. With any luck, she had a good shot at getting at least half of it done before the late afternoon crowd came straggling in to distract her.

But when she looked down at the still blank application spread out before her, her concentration wavered, allowing her thoughts to wander back to last night and Morgan's face when he'd admitted to wanting her as badly as she wanted him. In her ears, she heard again the twisted half-truths Gussy had read to her from the morning paper. She squeezed her eyes shut on a soft groan.

By now Morgan surely must have heard the news, she thought dully. Since she hadn't heard from him, it was all too apparent what his reaction had been. He wouldn't be able to protest without appearing guilty as sin, so that left him with only one recourse...ignore the column and the speculations it generated, ignore her.

It was for the best, she told herself. If he wasn't around to tempt her, it would be easier for her to stick to her resolve and to get out of his life once and for all. She should have been pleased. But all she wanted to do was cry. Swearing, she tossed down her pencil and gave up all pretense of working. What was the point? She wasn't fooling anybody, least of all herself. She hurt, and ignoring the pain wouldn't make it go away. Rising abruptly to her feet, she strode over to the tiny window that overlooked the parking lot and stared blindly out at the street before her.

She was still standing there, hugging herself, when Morgan stepped into the open doorway of her office. Hungrily, his eyes roamed over her. Dressed in jeans and a pink cowl-necked sweater, her hair pulled back in a ponytail, she was lost in thought, her face half-turned away from him, her expression pensive. He didn't have to ask if she'd seen the paper. Her shoulders drooped as if they held the weight of the world.

He felt his heart twist at the sight of her and almost went to her without a word, just needing to hold her. But he was here to tell her goodbye, and it was tearing him apart. Dear God, how had she become such an important part of his life so quickly? He'd known from the beginning she didn't fit in with his plans. She dragged him to places he never intended to go, got him involved with people who needed him more than he wanted to be needed. But when he touched her, he felt as if he'd been waiting for her forever. Whatever there was between them wasn't over, he promised himself. How could it end when there was still so much left unsaid, unresolved?

Resisting the urge to close the distance between them, he stayed where he was and propped a shoulder against the doorjamb. "Got a minute?"

Startled, Philly whirled, her eyes drinking in the sight of him. As usual he was impeccably dressed, this time in a dove gray suit, pale pink shirt and flowered tie. But his eyes looked tired, his dark brown hair disheveled as if he'd run his fingers through it too many times to count. What was he doing here? Surely he'd seen the paper....

Her breath caught at the thought, the blood draining from her face. Oh God, what if he hadn't? What if he was here to take up where they had left off last night? He might not even know that the latest talk on Capitol Hill was of how he was being seduced into rethinking his stand on the funding bill. By her. He would be livid. And considering his suspicions of her when they'd first met, he might even believe it.

Her heart clenched painfully, she braced as if for a blow. "You shouldn't be here," she said stiffly, forcing herself to look him in the eye. Hot color climbed in her cheeks. "The paper...didn't you see—"

"I saw Sarah Connors's column," he broke in grimly. "I don't normally read such garbage, but it was kind of hard to ignore."

So he didn't believe it. Her knees almost buckled in relief. "You still shouldn't be here. You know what people are saying. What if someone sees you—"

He wanted to tell her he didn't give a damn what anyone thought, but they both knew that as long as he was an elected official, he was vulnerable to the talk on the streets. Especially in an election year. Pushing away from the doorjamb, he straightened. "My campaign manager and I had an emergency meeting this morning. He thinks this would be a good time for me to start stumping across the state instead of waiting for the election recess. I came to say goodbye."

Philly reached blindly for her chair, her fingers curling into its high back in search of support for her suddenly sagging knees. "I see," she said huskily. "When do you leave?"

"Within the hour. Tim's been on the phone all day rescheduling my itinerary, planning a real old-fashioned, whistle-stop whirl through the state. I think we're going to hit every wide spot in the road."

She should have wished him well and left it at that. After all, the snide gossip about them in the paper hadn't really changed anything. They'd been heading for this moment from the day they'd met. But she couldn't let him go. Not yet. "What about the funding bill?"

"There's another investigative hearing on it next week, then the vote a few days after that. I'll make a quick trip back for both of them."

She didn't have to ask how he would vote. She knew he hadn't changed his mind. And after Sarah Connors's innuendos, he couldn't switch sides without looking like he really did let his heart rule his head. Yet, even though she knew she was being stupid, she couldn't help feeling that his vote against something that was so important to her represented the last, final, irrevocable vote against them. She just wished it was over with so she could start putting it behind her.

She summoned up a smile that was pitifully weak but the best she could manage. "I guess there's nothing left to say, then, is there? You'll do what you have to do and that's that. End of story."

There was no accusation in her words, only a proud, weary acceptance that he had never heard from her before. He didn't like it. She was trying so hard to be philosophical in the face of defeat that he wanted to shake her. Did she think he wanted to vote against the shelter? Against her? The time he'd spent with her there had touched him in a way he hadn't expected, moved him in ways that would haunt him every time he passed a grate where lonely men clung to the only warmth available to them. He'd learned that just writing a check wasn't always enough, and because of that lesson, he would be a better congressman. But that didn't make the decisions he had to make any easier.

"Damn it, don't look at me like that!" he growled. "Don't you think I've tried to find another way out of this? But I've got to go with my conscience. There's only so much money, and it has to be used in a way that will help the most people. Like it or not, that means funneling it into programs that will stimulate the economy and create jobs." Unable to stop himself, he stepped toward her. "Honey, if there were any other way..."

But there wasn't, or he would have found it. Somehow, deep down, she had always know that. Fighting back tears, she suddenly wanted him gone, out of there, while she could still let him go. Squaring her shoulders, she shrugged. "We all do what we have to do. Don't worry about me, you've still got King to tackle. I hope you beat him by a landslide."

He buried his hands in his pockets to keep from reaching for her. "Thanks. I'm going to give it my best shot."

This time there truly was nothing left to say. Silence grew and stretched between them like a chasm that was too deep and wide to breach. Philly's heart thrummed in her ears so loudly she was sure he could hear it, too. Just go! she wanted to cry, but she couldn't get the words past her tight throat. As if he heard her, he hesitated, clearly torn, his eyes telling her things he wouldn't let himself say. Then, without another word, he turned on his heel and walked out of her life.

The next two weeks were the most miserable she had ever known. She threw herself into her work, spending an ungodly number of hours at the shelter each day, wearing herself out so that when she went home late each night she would be too exhausted to do anything but fall into bed and lose herself in sleep. It didn't work. The second her body stilled, the instant she dropped her guard, Morgan was there, walking through the dark chambers of her mind as if he owned them.

She tried telling herself she just needed time. Time to get over him, time to forget. It wasn't as if she were one of those women who couldn't function without a man. Before she'd ever heard of Morgan Stewart II, she'd been perfectly content with her life. She had friends, had had dates that never bordered on anything serious, and work. That used to be enough for her. It would be again.

But with every passing day her misery only seemed to get worse. Her appetite dwindled until it was nearly nonexistent, she lost weight she couldn't afford to lose, and restless nights carved violet circles under her eyes. She learned through the news that Morgan made two quick trips back to D.C. to attend committee hearings. And both times he was there and gone before she'd even known he was in town. He didn't call, of course. She hadn't expected him to. But it hurt, nonetheless.

Later, Philly never knew how much longer she could have gone on that way if Gussy hadn't intervened. She knew the older woman was worried about her—she never asked what had happened between her and Morgan, but she fussed and grumbled over her, pushing her to eat, to take some time off, to relax. When that didn't work, she took matters into her own hands and announced that they both needed to get out of town for a while. Without giving Philly time to so much as open her mouth, she arranged for someone to take over Philly's shift at the shelter, packed her bags for her and whisked her off to her beach house in Ocean City for the weekend.

The house was a far cry from Gussy's Bethesda mansion. A simple wood-frame structure built over a two-car garage a hundred yards from the water and a mile from town, there was no television or phone. The furniture was sturdy rather than elegant, the three bedrooms almost Spartan in their decor. A wide porch encircled the house on three sides, and large paned windows in every room offered tantalizing views of the ocean.

The nearest neighbor was three sand dunes away, but most of the other homes were boarded up for the winter and deserted. Unable to stay inside, Philly found herself drawn to the long, lonely stretches of the beach. There the only sounds were the cry of the gulls searching for food, the moan of the wind tugging at her hair, the ever present rush of the waves breaking on the sand and the echo of her thoughts dodging her footsteps. She walked for miles.

Gussy had brought her there to find some peace, and for a while she did. The salt air filled her lungs and stung her cheeks with color, and for the first time in two weeks, she was actually hungry at supper. Afterward, she and Gussy lit a fire in the old-fashioned potbellied stove in the living room and sat talking for hours about anything and everything. Except Morgan. By unspoken agreement his name was off-limits.

By the time they both retired, it was nearly midnight. Turning out her bedroom light, Philly crawled into bed and stretched out under an old patchwork quilt with a tired sigh. Outside the wind whistled around the corner of the house while the waves continued to pound the beach. She should have been lulled into sleep just by closing her eyes. But as her body relaxed, her mind opened to the memories she'd been running from all day. Morgan was a hundred miles away, but against her closed eyelids, she could see the wicked curve of his mouth as clearly as if he stood directly before her. Tears burned her throat. Would there ever come a night when she wouldn't dream of the man?

Lost in her misery, it was a long moment before she heard what sounded like a footstep on the wooden stairs that led from the porch down to the beach and the garage under the house. She froze, her heart suddenly pounding. She must have been mistaken, she told herself. There was no one around but her and Gussy. Maybe the house was just settling. Or a raccoon or coyote was checking out the garbage cans.

Then she heard it again. A footstep. A definite footstep and too heavy to be anything but a man's. Dear God, someone was coming up the stairs! Panic squeezed her throat with cold fingers. She had to do something! She couldn't just lie there and wait to be murdered in her bed! Tossing off the covers, she reached for her robe with shaking fingers.

Nine

Fumbling blindly in the dark, Morgan searched the ledge over the front door for the key Gussy always kept hidden there despite warnings that it was an open invitation to any burglar who happened to come across it. But all his seeking fingers encountered was a grimy coating of sand. "Hell," he muttered under his breath. Dropping his hands, he stepped back to glare at the locked door. What the devil had she done with the damn thing? If he wasn't so tired, he'd drive to the nearest phone and call her.

And end up asking her about Philly, he thought grimly. He wouldn't be able to stop himself. For the last two weeks he'd thrown himself into the campaign with a fierceness that had delighted Tim, but it was Philly he thought of when he made every impassioned speech, Philly he saw in the faces of the crowds that grew larger every day, Philly he dreamed about in one lonely hotel room after another, night after night. All of his energy should have been focused on pulling away from King, but the only thing he could think about was how he would have given up ten points in the damn polls just to hear the sound of her voice.

One reason, he thought, his mouth pressed flat in a harsh line. He needed only one reason to get back in his car and drive half the night to see her, to hold her, to make love to her. If he called Gussy now, she just might give him that reason. Resisting the lure of the stairs that led down to his car and the nearest phone, he set his jaw determinedly and started checking the windows.

Philly silently crept down the darkened hall on cold, bare feet, her hand soundlessly sliding along the wall to guide her way to the living room, her eyes wide with fright. She was just going to peek and see what they were up against, she told herself, then wake up Gussy. From the front porch she thought she heard a sound at the door, the whisper of the knob turning, the lock holding, a man's low, muttered curse carried away by the wind. Her heart slammed against her ribs. What if he had a gun? she thought suddenly, paling. She and Gussy would be defenseless against whatever depravity he was capable of. They had to get away! Now, before he even knew they were there...

She started to turn back toward Gussy's bedroom at the far end of the hall but froze at the sound of a living room window slowly being eased open. Her blood iced over in her veins. *Run!* a voice screamed in her head, but she couldn't. The minute he climbed through the window, he only had to look up to see her pale figure running down the hall.

She didn't stop to think, but acted on pure instinct. Hurrying over to the potbellied stove, she snatched up a small log from the firewood stacked in a neat pile nearby and clutched it like a club. Between one heartbeat and the next, she soundlessly darted to the window and positioned herself out of sight next to it.

A second passed, then another, dragging like years and giving her too much time to think. Her palms dampened, her breath began to sough through her lungs, and she was afraid she was going to wimp out when it came down to the crunch. Then a long masculine leg was sliding through the open window, followed by a dark head and broad shoulders, and she did what every TV hero did in a similar situation. She raised the log to brain him and cried, "Freeze!"

"What the hell—"

She would have known that irritated voice from the other side of the moon. Horrified, she dropped the log from suddenly numb fingers. "Morgan?"

Her hoarse whisper went through him like a rifle shot. Still caught on the windowsill, he froze, his head snapping up to find her in the dark. "*Philly?* My God, what are you doing here?"

It wasn't the most joyous greeting she'd ever heard. In fact, he sounded almost accusing, as if she were the last person on earth he wanted to see. And after she'd spent two weeks crying her heart out over him, she thought bitterly. How quickly things changed. Suddenly cold, she tugged her robe tighter around her.

"Gussy wanted to get away for the weekend," she said in a low, flat voice that wouldn't carry beyond the living room and wake the older woman. "Obviously you did, too. I'll try to stay out of your way. Unless you led a trail of reporters here, I don't think you have to worry about anyone seeing us together. There's no one around but the gulls. Good night."

She heard him swear, felt him reach for her as he quickly climbed the rest of the way inside. But she slipped by him in the dark and hurried down the hall, her bare feet making only a whisper of sound, the delicate softness of her pink-and-white robe a blur in the night. She promised herself she wouldn't cry; she wouldn't give in to the hurt clawing her heart. But the second she made the sanctuary of her room, her vision clouded. A hot tear spilled over her lashes. Then another. Muttering a curse, she dashed them away.

Behind her the door opened quietly. Her heart stumbled to a halt, only to jerk into a rapid, uneven rhythm. Turning to face him, she saw only a tall, dark shadow in the doorway, his eyes gleaming with purpose as they met hers. "I don't know what you think you're doing, but this is no time of the night for games," she said stiffly. "Go to your own room."

For an answer, he stepped further into the room and shut the door behind him.

"Damn it, Morgan, I mean it—"

His teeth flashed in the darkness in an ironic grin. "This is my room."

She blinked. "What?"

"This is my room. Always has been since I was a kid. You can hear the water better here than at the back of the house. That's why I chose it."

That was why she'd chosen it, too, but she had no intention of telling him that. "Fine," she snapped. "Then it's all yours. I'll take the room next door."

She started around him but had barely drawn even with him when his hand snaked out to grab her arm. "Stay."

He spoke the single word in little more than a hoarse whisper, yet she gasped as if he'd shouted the request to the rooftops. Every pulse in her body seemed to still, to wait. The tears that she'd just barely regained control of welled up again, burning her throat, thickening her voice. Without even realizing it, she shook her head, denying herself, denying them both. "Don't do this to me. Please, just go...."

"Don't you think I tried that?" he murmured, slowly drawing her closer. "I promised myself I wasn't coming within fifty miles of you. I wasn't going to call you. I wasn't even going to mention your name when I checked in with Gussy to see how she was doing." His hands, always so sure, so steady, trembled as they gently pushed her dark cloud of hair back from her face. "But I missed you. God, how I missed you! I dreamed of you so much I started to dread going to bed at night because I couldn't get you out of my head."

So it had been the same for him. Closing her eyes against the sweet ache he generated with nothing more than words, she wanted to tell him to stop, but his hands settled on her shoulders, stroking, gliding up her neck to the sensitive hollow behind her ear, then slowly trailing back down again, relearning the shape of her, the feel of her. Suddenly, instead of pushing him away, her hands were latching on to his waist, holding on to him for dear life. "I know," she choked. "It was the same for me."

"Tonight was the worst," he confided thickly. Before she could guess his intentions, he swooped down and found her mouth in the dark. As far as kisses went, it wasn't an earth-shattering one. Hardly longer than a heartbeat, a tickle of mustache, a dry brush of lips. But its roughness spoke of a hunger that burned, the clench of his hands dragging her closer out of a yearning that had pushed his control to the edge. "It just all seemed to come to a head," he muttered, nipping at her lips, "and I knew if I didn't find myself some peace, I'd be knocking at your apartment door before dawn. So I came here."

The hands at her throat somehow found their way inside her robe and she never thought to wonder how. Heat licked at her, melting her knees. Hot fingers traced the neckline of her gown, dipping down between her breasts, dragging a moan from her. "I thought you didn't want me here," she cried softly, clinging to what little reason she had left. "You sounded as if I were the last person on earth you wanted to see."

"Ah, sweetheart, you were the only one I wanted to see." Trailing kisses over her cheeks, her chin, against her closed eyes, he filled his hands with the satin wildness of her hair and leaned his forehead against hers, his breath a hot, moist caress against her throbbing lips as he softly urged her to open her eyes. "Some things are a gift from the gods," he whispered in a voice as rough as sandpaper when she finally lifted her dazed gaze to his. "Call it Fate, Kismet, whatever. We're here, together, and nothing else seems to matter. Let me make love to you."

It was a request, not a demand, the decision all hers. All she had to do was say no and she knew he would release her and find the strength to walk away. Her heart lurched painfully at the thought. Clutching at him, she searched his face in the opaque shadows that wrapped around them, closing out the world.

He made no promises in the dark and didn't even hint about the future, which was no more than she'd expected. They both knew giving in to their need for each other wasn't going to change all the differences that drove a wedge between them. But they could have tonight. Two weeks ago, it was more than either of them had thought they could have.

"Morgan..."

She said nothing more than his name, and that so low he had to bend his head to catch it. But her voice was raw with need, honeyed with acceptance, sweet with a longing that he would carry with him to his grave. Overwhelmed by a tenderness that staggered him, he brought his mouth to hers.

He kissed her as if she were the most precious thing in the world, held her as if she were more delicate than the finest spun glass, touched her with a gentleness that should have told her more clearly than words that he meant to linger and savor, to test and tease, to commit every inch of her to memory until they were both out of their minds with wanting. Tonight was theirs. And he was going to drag out every second of it.

It should have been easy for him. He knew how to pleasure a woman, how to keep a tight rein on his own desires until he brought her to the brink of release, then tumble them both over into satisfaction. But all his experience, all of his self-control, counted for squat when it came to Philly.

Alone in the dark with her, with the wind moaning around the corners of the house and the waves beating, always beating, at the beach, she went to his head like a fifth of whiskey. He tried to keep his kisses slow and gentle, intending to deepen them gradually, but she would have none of it. Her arms climbed around his neck, her sweet, hungry mouth turned blindly up to his and her tongue shyly, then boldly mated with his. The gentleness in him burned up on a wave of heat that raised the temperature in his loins ten degrees.

His hands tightened and pulled her flush against his arousal before he could stop himself. *Too fast,* he told himself. You're going too fast, Stewart. Swearing, he wrenched his mouth from hers, his breath tearing through his lungs, but he couldn't force his hands to abandon their exploration of the soft, enticing curves hidden under her nightclothes. A heartbeat later her robe slid down her body to pool at her feet even as he growled against her neck, "Easy, honey. We've got all night."

He might as well have saved his breath. Tugging his mouth back down to hers, she gave him a kiss that rocked him back on his heels, then attacked his clothes

with a desperation that seemed to surprise her as much
as it did him. Tugging his tie free, she sent it sailing
with a total disregard for its cost. His coat followed,
then his shirt, baring him to her seeking hands. Murmuring against his mouth, she sent her fingers running over his chest, his collarbone, testing the hard
strength of his muscles, the responsiveness of his flat
male nipples.

That was when his good intentions went straight to
hell. Growling low in his throat, he ripped her nightgown from her and attacked the zipper of his slacks.
He never even remembered kicking off his shoes or
peeling off his underwear and socks. A flat two seconds later, he had them both right where he wanted
them—bare as the day they were born and in bed.
God, the nights he had dreamed of this!

But this was no dream. This was a fantasy come to
life. The room was as black as pitch and they could see
little more than the gleam of desire in each other's
eyes. But the darkness only intensified their senses,
making a touch more potent than an all-out assault, a
whisper more stirring than a wild cry of longing. Time
ceased to exist; inhibitions were stripped away,
thought forgotten. The sheets could have caught fire
and neither would have noticed or cared.

The night darkened, heated, thickened with need.
But this was a need that Morgan was unfamiliar with,
a need that coiled and burned and threatened to turn
him inside out. He felt her shudder when he took her
nipple into his mouth to tease and torment, felt her
gasp as he traced every sweet curve of her with his
tongue, felt her melt and dissolve when his fingers

found the hot, damp, womanly folds of her. But still it wasn't enough. With nothing more than the gentle exploration of her hands, she pushed him to boundaries of desire. Then her lips blindly roamed the length of him, tasting, caressing, and he realized that nothing he had ever experienced before could have prepared him for this. For Philly.

The last of his control splintered. His hands tightened on her, sweeping her beneath him, opening her for him. He meant to take her then, to end this gnawing ache that burned hotter than any fire, but she wanted no part of taking, only giving. With a hunger as strong as his own, she took him into her and gave...everything. Heart, soul, sweetness and fire, she held nothing back, moving with him, against him, for him, racing with him to the beckoning edge of the unknown. But even then she didn't stop. Her thighs locked tight around his hips, holding him as if she would never let him go, she didn't hesitate, didn't once check her pace. His name a shattered cry upon her lips, she fell headlong into ecstasy and pulled him after her into the flames that licked at his soul.

The raucous shriek of a gull cut through the quiet stillness of the morning. Lying flat on her stomach, her head half-buried under her pillow, Philly stirred, then burrowed deeper into the covers, her eyes closed tight against the too bright sunlight that crept in past the drawn drapes covering the windows. Against her closed eyelids hazy images flickered, barely registering on her sleep-shrouded mind—Morgan, kissing her, stripping her nightgown from her, pulling her down to _ the bed and loving her as if his very sanity had depended on having her. A dream, she thought mistily. She was having the most wonderful dream. Murmuring his name, she reached for him.

And felt her bare breasts, sensitized from a night of loving, rub against the sheets. Her eyes popped open. She was naked! How... Her startled gaze fell on the pink-and-white gauzy puddle on the floor that was her gown and robe, and memories of the night came flooding back on a tide of heat, warming her. Hugging her pillow to her, she closed her eyes and lay perfectly still, letting herself remember the sweetness, the fire, the drugging pleasure that had weighted her limbs and sent her soaring into the stars at one and the same time. And his voice, she thought dreamily. Would she ever crawl into bed again without hearing his low, husky murmur in her ear, whispering encouraging, erotic words and promises that even now, hours later, could melt her bones?

Whenever she'd allowed herself to think of making love with him, she'd been so sure she knew what to expect. The flash and sizzle of a thunderstorm that comes out of nowhere and sweeps you along in its path, giving you no time to think, no time to protect your heart, no time to do anything but feel. Yet it had turned out to be so much more than that.

Tenderness. How could she have known that the smooth, suave, experienced playboy congressman had so much tenderness in him that his hands would shake with it when he took her? Even when he'd been rough, nearly out of control, there had been an underlying gentleness in his touch that had brought tears to her eyes. He'd promised her one night of sex, then given her a glimpse of what it would be like to be cherished by him, loved by him.

A month from now, a year down the road, the memory of their lovemaking would warm many long, cold, lonely nights. But for now, all she could think of was that he'd left without ever knowing that the few precious hours he'd given her would never be enough. She loved him; she could no longer deny it. And she would never be satisfied with spending anything less than eternity with him. But eternity was out of reach.

A lump of tears gathered in her throat, almost choking her. Swallowing thickly, she buried her face in her pillow and gave serious consideration to pulling the covers over her head and spending the rest of the day in bed crying her eyes out. But even if she'd been one to give in to misery—which she wasn't— there was Gussy to consider. She'd be worried sick about her if she holed up in her room all day. Sighing in defeat, she reached for her robe and headed for the bathroom and a shower, feeling utterly weary.

Thirty minutes later, comfortably dressed in old cords and a red flannel shirt that was two sizes too big, she made her way to the kitchen and started breakfast. Her mind carefully blank, she did the dishes she and Gussy had been too tired to do the previous night, put on a pot of coffee to brew and whipped up enough pancakes to feed a small army. By the time Gussy appeared in the doorway in a blue quilted robe, her face freshly washed and her white hair neatly combed, she had the table set, butter and syrup within reach, and the coffee ready to pour.

"Just in time," Philly greeted her, pasting on a light, carefree smile. Flicking off the burner under the griddle, she scooped up the overflowing platter of pancakes and carried it to the small dinette in the breakfast nook. "Hope you're hungry. I sort of got carried away."

"I'll say." Gussy chuckled, but her eyes were on Philly's pale, drawn face as she took the seat across from her at the table. "Were you expecting company?"

"No one but the gulls. They'll probably be thrilled to get the leftovers." Suddenly noticing that the juice glasses she'd set out earlier were still empty, she popped up from her seat. "Oops, forgot the orange juice. And the coffee. I don't know about you, but I need some caffeine to get me moving this morning."

She was already moving about like a nervous lightning bug, fluttering about the kitchen as if she couldn't sit still, chattering about anything and everything but what was on her mind, making no attempt to even taste the pancakes she'd piled on her plate. Worried, Gussy watched her through narrowed eyes and held her tongue as long as she could. When Philly started on a second cup of coffee, she said quietly, "I was hoping you could convince Morgan to spend the rest of the weekend with us. He needs a break."

Her coffee cup at her lips, Philly almost scalded her tongue. Swearing under her breath, she set the cup down with a thud. "You knew he was here?"

She nodded, a half smile curling the corners of her mouth. "I did the same thing you did—got up to see who was breaking into the house. When I saw it was Morgan, I thought you two could use some time together, so I went back to bed." Reaching across the table, she patted her hand. "I'm so glad you're working things out. I always knew you two were perfect for each other."

Torn between laughter and tears, Philly choked out, "Then you're the only one who does. Damn it Gussy, if we're seen together, I could cost him the election! Because of me, his ethics are being questioned for the first time in his career. How can we possibly be perfect for each other?"

"Do you like him?"

She blinked at the abrupt sharpness of the question. "I love him!"

"But do you like him? Forget the petty differences—the differences in your backgrounds and lifestyles, the fact that you act on your feelings and he never makes a move without being logical. Do you like the man? What he is? What he stands for?"

"Of course."

Gussy grinned, satisfied. "Then all the rest is just bull. You like him, you love him, you respect him. Some people spend a lifetime searching for what you've already got. Considering that, how can anything else matter?"

Philly wanted desperately to believe her, but she couldn't. She just couldn't take the risk. She was already hurting. If she let herself start to hope that they really could have a future together and it fell through, she'd be shattered. "Nothing's that simple," she whispered. "It can't be."

Gussy could have argued further, but she only patted her hand again and confided, "By the time you get to be my age, you'll know that life can be as simple or as complicated as you want it to be. A problem is only a problem if you let it become one. The choice is up to you."

The choice is up to you.

Seated on the floor before the potbellied stove, her arms clasping her drawn-up knees, Philly nearly groaned as Gussy's words echoed in her head for what must have been the thousandth time since breakfast. She'd spent the day ignoring them, denying them, refusing to allow the kind of thinking that could set her up for the biggest fall of her life. She actually thought she'd succeeded until evening arrived and the shadows grew longer, deeper.

Then hope slipped in under the cover of darkness, stealing into her heart. Unconsciously she found herself looking for Morgan's headlights down the road, listening for his step on the stairs. Gussy turned in at eleven, the house settled and grew quiet. Midnight came and went. Still she sat before the fire. Waiting.

At ten to one she forced herself to accept the inevitable. He wasn't coming, had never intended to come. If she'd listened to her head instead of her heart, she'd have been asleep hours ago. Ridiculously hurt, she switched off the lights and headed for her room.

But the minute her eyes landed on the bed, she knew she couldn't do it. She couldn't crawl back between sheets that still held his scent and find any peace. Wanting, needing to cry, she snatched up her gown and bolted into the connecting bathroom and turned on the shower. But even when she was stripped bare and standing under the hot, pulsing spray, the tears wouldn't come.

She never knew how long she'd been standing there, letting the water pound away at her pain, when she thought she heard a soft knock at the bathroom door. Her heart stumbled. She tried to tell herself he wouldn't come this late, but her hand was already sweeping back the shower curtain. The streaming water forgotten, she started to reach for a towel, but she never had a chance. The door opened, and suddenly he was there before her.

Morgan stopped dead at the sight of her, his eyes devouring her. Last night his hands and mouth had explored every inch of her, but the darkness had concealed the creaminess of her skin, the perky tilt of her breasts with their rosy tips, the dark, tempting thatch of curls at the juncture of her thighs. Beaded with water, her long wet hair clinging to her while a mist of steam rose around her, she was the most beautiful woman he had ever seen.

With an abrupt, stiff movement, he jerked off his tie. "I tried to stay away," he rasped, never taking his hot gaze from her as he shrugged out of his coat and attacked the buttons of his shirt. "Eleven hours from now I've got to be in D.C. for one last committee meeting on the shelter funding bill. The day after that we vote on it." His shirt hit the floor, then his belt, shoes and socks. "I told myself to wait till then to see you because I wouldn't be forced into choosing between you and what I have to do."

His zipper grated down almost angrily, the sound matching the tempest burning in his eyes. "But, damn it, I couldn't stay away." In one savage movement, his pants and underwear joined the pile of discarded clothes on the floor and he was stalking toward her, making no attempt to hide his arousal from her. "You're all I thought about all day."

The words were accusing, furious, frustrated. But when he stepped into the tub and snapped the shower curtain closed, his hands were shaking with need as he wrapped her tight against him. Water sluiced over him, instantly drenching him, but he only groaned and hugged her closer. "God, I don't want to lose you!"

The surprise that had held her motionless before him snapped. Her arms curved around him, her hands climbing his bare back, holding him as if she would never let him go. His name a ragged sigh on her lips, she rubbed her cheek back and forth against the hard muscles of his chest, the tears that had refused to fall all day spilling over her lashes to hide in the water that already ran down her cheeks. "I don't want to lose you, either, but—"

"To hell with buts!" he growled, and nudged her chin up to take her mouth in a hot, thorough, knee-weakening kiss that drove every thought but that of him from her mind. He kissed her as if they had forever . . . forever to tease, to entice, to woo, as if it were the first time, the sweetest time. With lips and teeth and tongue he played and seduced, showing her all the different ways a man could destroy a woman's reason with nothing more than a kiss.

She was clinging to him when he finally tore his mouth from hers. Pliant, boneless in his arms, her cheeks flushed and her eyelids too heavy to lift, she groaned in protest and tried to bring his lips back to hers. Drawing back only far enough to take in all of her with a single glance, Morgan knew he would always remember her just as she was at that moment. Wet and supple, her sodden black hair streaming down her bare back, her lips parted and swollen from his kisses, every soft, delicate curve of her body perfectly aligned with his.

The heat in his loins burned hotter, urging him to take her like some primitive man reclaiming what was his. But it was too soon, much too soon for the type of loving he wanted tonight. Forcing himself to relax, his fingers glided over her slick skin with tantalizing slowness.

Philly shuddered, need streaking through her. The water beat down on them in a never-ending cascade, but all she could feel was the butterfly touch of his hands tracing her bare shoulders, testing the weight of her breasts, the pout of a nipple, trailing fire down the center of her body to the heat of her desire. Crying out his name, she swayed against him, the sensations drugging her sharpening abruptly into a desire that threatened to shatter her into a million pieces.

But Morgan hadn't even begun his sweet torture. Everywhere his hands had touched, his mouth followed. Murmuring her name over and over again, he drank the moisture from her skin and touched his tongue to her with maddening slowness. Breasts, stomach, thighs and everything in between. Lowering his dark head to her pale, translucent skin, he teased, tormented and took with ever-increasing hunger, letting the pleasure build.

By the time he retraced his path back up her quivering body, she was lost, boneless, his to do with as he willed. His own body screaming for release, he started to sweep her up into his arms and carry her to bed while he could still manage to walk. But she stopped him with a single word. "No."

What patience he had left threatened to unravel. "Honey—"

"Here," she urged desperately, reaching for him, her heart pounding and blood raging. "Take me here. Now."

She tossed her head back, unmindful of the shower's spray, her green eyes full of passion and a daring he couldn't resist. She could have asked for the moon right then, and he'd have searched heaven and hell for a way to get it for her. Groaning her name, he did as she demanded and took her.

Ten

For the fifth time in three minutes, Philly glanced at her watch, swore and resumed pacing the length of her living room. In ten minutes the Appropriation Committee would meet for its final vote on the funding bill. Ten minutes, she thought numbly. That was all the time she had left to hang on to a dream that just wasn't meant to be. Ever since Morgan had left her at dawn yesterday to rush back to D.C., she'd told herself she was prepared for it; she could handle it. But with every hated tick of the clock, she knew she was lying.

She had, in fact, been lying to herself from the moment she'd fallen at his feet and unknowingly started the long, heady tumble into love. She'd been so sure she could accept the hand Fate had dealt her, that if she couldn't have forever with him, she could still be content with the here and now. Like a naive fool she'd thought she could love him without restraints, then let him go when the time came, without regret.

How could she have known the hurt she was setting herself up for? she wondered, swallowing a sob. The heartache? She'd thought she'd known what love was, but nothing in her experience came close to the agony she was feeling now. And Morgan hadn't even cast his vote yet. The real pain hadn't begun. Dear God, how was she going to stand it?

Hugging herself, she wandered to the front windows of her apartment and stared out at the grim, overcast day. As if drawn by a magnet, her tortured gaze locked on the clean, elegant lines of the Stewart mansion, which sat in stately splendor fifty yards away, surrounded by acres of lightly wooded estate that kept a full-time gardener busy year-round. Would she ever be able to look at the house again without looking for Morgan? she wondered, blinking back stupid tears. Would she ever be able to step into the kitchen for a cozy tea with Gussy without waiting for him to walk in the back door? Because she knew he would. One day when she least expected it, she'd look up and he'd be standing directly in front of her.

She couldn't stay here.

The realization came to her quickly, coldly, filling her with stark despair. She couldn't spend her days and nights waiting for chance encounters with him, unconsciously living for those few precious moments when their eyes would meet and time would stand still. Better to completely cut herself out of his life once and for all than be reduced to that.

The decision made, she made herself turn from the window before she could find a reason to change her mind. There was nothing left to do but pack.

Morgan blinked as if he hadn't heard correctly, his fingers unconsciously tightening on the phone. "What do you mean, she's gone? Gone where?"

"I don't know." Her lined face grim, Gussy stared out her kitchen windows at the deserted apartment over the garage. "She came in thirty minutes ago and said she couldn't stay here any longer. I tried reasoning with her, but she already had her mind made up and bags loaded in her car. She wouldn't even tell me what was wrong, just that she had to leave."

Stunned, Morgan sank against a corner of his desk, his mind reeling. Gone, he thought hollowly. How could she be gone? Damn it, he had news to share with her, news that he'd been on his way to tell her when Gussy's call had caught him at his office just as he was walking out the door. She couldn't be gone, just like that, without a word. Not after what they'd shared at the beach house. He loved her!

Why had it taken him so long to see it? For weeks he hadn't been able to eat or sleep or dream without thinking of her. When he should have been focusing all of his attention on King, he'd found himself continually distracted by a pair of dancing green eyes and a sassy grin instead. And the loneliness she'd revealed to him! God, would he ever forget what it was like to be hundreds of miles from her and aching for the election to be over and done with just so that he could be with her?

He should have realized then that he was in love with her, but it wasn't until he'd spent two incredible nights with her that it hit him. What they'd shared had been so much more than mere lust, so much more than physical. Somehow she'd captured a part of his soul and claimed it for eternity, and he'd known nothing would ever be the same again. Leaving her had been pure hell, but he'd promised himself that it was for the last time. And come hell or high water, he would find a way to vote for the funding bill without having to abandon his convictions.

Damn it, he'd done that, but it was too late. She was gone. How could she have just turned her back and walked away from him? "She must have said something else," he insisted hoarsely. "What about her job at the shelter? I can't believe she'd just quit that without notice."

"She didn't mention the shelter. She just told me to tell you goodbye and that she'd be pulling for you to win the election."

He swore then, a string of muttered, self-directed expletives that would have done a sailor proud. Gussy winced. "What are you going to do?"

"Do?" he echoed sharply. "I'm going to find her, that's what. And then I'm going to marry her."

But when he hung the phone up, he knew it might not be as easy as that. Just finding her could be difficult if she decided to drop out of his life completely. She'd already proven herself to be a woman who wasn't interested in material things; and she worked with people every day who had walked away from homes, families, friends, and lost themselves in the streets, never to be heard from again. If she wanted to, she could find work at one of a thousand shelters across the country, volunteer her services in exchange for food and a bed, and simply disappear.

His steely eyes glinted with determination. She could run as fast and as far as she liked, but he wasn't letting her give up on what they could have together. His face drawn, he reached for the phone.

Gary stood in the doorway of Philly's office and watched her with dark, worried eyes. Without a word of explanation, she'd arrived at the shelter an hour ago with everything she owned stowed in her car. Pale and quiet, she'd announced she would be spending the night there, then find herself another apartment tomorrow. Something was obviously very wrong, but she hadn't given him the chance to ask what. Instead she'd retreated to her office with the excuse that she had paperwork to catch up on.

Her head was bowed over her desk, the hand holding her pencil steady as it moved across the paper spread out before her, but every time she looked up, her eyes were lost and bruised with hurt. Gary wanted to tell her she was fooling no one but herself, but he held his tongue, knowing she would talk when she was ready.

"You should be out celebrating instead of hiding behind that desk," he said quietly. "You won."

She glanced up, a frown carving a groove between her brows. "Won what? What are you talking about?"

A half grin propped up one corner of his mouth. "The funding bill. I just heard the news on the radio. The Appropriation Committee passed it unanimously."

The pencil she was holding fell heedlessly from her suddenly numb fingers. "Unanimously," she echoed, confused. "But how? Morgan—"

For the first time since her unexpected arrival, Gary saw something other than pain in her eyes. Relieved, he explained, "It seems the good Congressman has spent the last two days hammering out a compromise. He got the other committee members to agree to increase funding with the stipulation that the states had to provide matching funds for job training."

For one unguarded moment elation skyrocketed through her. He'd done it! Morgan had found a way to get the job training he'd promised his constituents without turning her people out into the cold. Oh, God, she should have trusted him! She should have known that he wouldn't vote against something that was so important to her without trying to find a compromise they could both live with. She had to call him—

Her hand stopped halfway to the phone, reality slapping her in the face. What good would calling him do? Nothing had changed. The funding bill had been only one of their problems. Eliminating it didn't eliminate the fact that they wanted two different things out of life. She would always bring home strays and people in need and give them the shirt off her back if necessary. One day he, like his grandfather before him, would be Speaker of the House. The two were not compatible.

Instead of reaching for the phone, she picked up her pencil, her fingers gripping it until her knuckles were white. "That's wonderful," she said stiffly. "Looks like the nights Stewart worked here paid off after all."

Without another word, she turned her attention back to her work. Gary's brows snapped into a bewildered frown. "Is that all you have to say about it?"

She never lifted her gaze from the report in front of her. "What else is there to say? The money will certainly help, but it'll take more than federal funds to keep our doors open. Which is why I'm working on this plan to increase private and corporate donations," she said, finally glancing up to shoot him a meaningful glance. "I plan to present it to the board next week, so I've got my work cut out for me."

She saw him hesitate, his frown deepen into a scowl as he fought with the obvious need to say something. Hating herself for rejecting his concern when he had always been such a good friend to her, she didn't offer him a word of encouragement. Swearing softly, he said, "Well, then, I'll let you get back to it."

She almost called him back when he turned and walked out, but then the phone rang and drove every other thought from her head. She stared at it, dread backing up in her throat. She didn't have to answer it to know it was Morgan. She hadn't asked Gussy to keep her leave-taking a secret, even though she'd known the older woman would probably call Morgan the minute he returned to his office from voting on the funding bill. Philly had been waiting for his call for the past half hour.

Bracing herself for the confrontation that was sure to come, she picked up the phone and said coolly, "Franklin Shelter for the Homeless. Philadelphia O'Neil speaking. May I help you?"

Relief coursed through Morgan at the sound of her voice. "What you can do is tell me what the hell you mean by moving out of Gussy's," he growled. "Damn it, Philly, why? You didn't even wait for the vote before you left."

He made no attempt to hide his hurt, his pain, his accusing tone stabbing her in the heart. Tears flooded her eyes. "Morgan, please, don't."

"Don't? Don't what? Don't jump to the conclusion that you're kicking me out of your life? That you're walking away from what we could have together without even giving me a chance to make it work? Damn it, woman, *I love you!*"

He fairly shouted the words at her, then could have kicked himself. Imbecile! You didn't tell a woman you loved her for the first time by yelling it at her over the phone! Swearing under his breath, he struggled for the control that had never been shattered until she'd come into his life. "Honey, please, I didn't mean to do this over the phone. I'm coming over—"

"No!"

"Sweetheart, don't be ridiculous. You can't expect me to tell you I love you, then leave it at that. I'll be right over—"

"If you do, I won't be here."

The words were spoken no louder than a whisper, but they stopped Morgan in his tracks. She meant it, he thought dazedly. If he pushed her now, he'd lose her forever. "Don't try to convince me you don't love me," he said quietly. "I won't believe you."

Silence echoed across the line, stretching his nerves to the breaking point before she admitted in a voice strangled by tears, "No, I love you. But sometimes love isn't enough."

"Why the hell not? It's the only thing that matters. My God, honey, don't you know I've been looking a lifetime for you? How can you say what we have isn't enough?"

"Because in the real world, Prince Charming can't sweep Cinderella off to the castle and expect her to fit in," she said sadly. "It would never work."

"I've seen you dressed to the nines," he argued gruffly. "You can fit in anywhere, sweetheart."

"But I don't belong there. I belong on skid row helping the people who have no one else to help them. Don't you see? In my world, when someone is hungry, you give them food. If they're cold, you don't ask questions. You ask them inside and give them a blanket. In yours, as a congressman, you have to ask who else needs food, who needs it the most and who might be able to pay. Nothing can be given freely, instantly, without hearings and arguments and discussions. In the end, it takes Congress months to do what I can do overnight. How can we possibly be compatible when your work creates the very red tape that constantly ties my hands in mine?"

He wanted to tell her they'd find a way to work everything out if she'd just give them a chance, but she was in no mood to listen to reason now. "Obviously we're not going to get anywhere talking about this on the phone. And since you won't let me come over, there's not much else to say. Except that I'm giving you fair warning here and now that this conversation isn't over. And next time we discuss us, sweetheart, I will be in the same room, with you. That's a promise."

Her heart pounding, Philly opened her mouth to tell him there would be no next time, but he never gave her the chance. With a quiet click, he hung up.

The last two weeks of the campaign stretched out before Morgan like an eternity. Every day was booked to the hilt, planned right down the last minute. Time was short and tempers were even shorter, and the tension mounted. From city to town to wide spot in the road, he spoke to thousands of people, shook hands with nameless, faceless undecideds whose vote held the key to victory. He forgot the number of babies he kissed, the number of tasteless rubber chickens he forced down at fund-raisers, the speeches he gave to anyone who would listen. Sometimes he was so tired at night that he even forgot what town he was in when he finally dropped into bed. But he never forgot to call Philly.

She didn't want to talk to him. When she answered the phone at the shelter the first three nights he was gone, he could almost hear her stiffen when she recognized his voice, bracing herself for a repeat of the conversation they'd had the day she moved out of Gussy's. But he didn't talk about anything more personal than the campaign, her day, the weather. Wishing he could be with her there, working side by side with her again, he promised himself he would be when the madness of the campaign was over with.

Gradually she would relax and even laugh with him, while their voices dropped to whispers that spoke of things that were never said. It wasn't what he wanted, but all he could have for the moment. At least he could fall asleep at night knowing he could reach her just by stretching out his arm and picking up the phone.

Then the fourth night, Gary answered the phone, his harried "Franklin Shelter" raised to nearly a shout in order to be heard over the loud, unhappy cries of a baby in the background.

The receiver caught between his ear and shoulder as he sat on the side of his bed and unbuttoned his shirt, Morgan stiffened, uneasiness stirring in him. But he only said lightly, "Hi, Gary, this is Morgan. Sounds like you've got your hands full there. Is this a bad time for Philly to come to the phone?"

The other man hesitated, then reluctantly said, "I'm sorry, man, but she's not here. She moved into an apartment today."

Without once warning him last night that she wouldn't be there the next time he called, Morgan thought as hurt ripped through his gut like a rusty knife. If he could have gotten his hands on her at that moment, he'd have been tempted to shake her until her teeth rattled, then sweep her off to bed and show her that what they had was something she couldn't keep running from. But they were a hundred and fifty miles apart and there wasn't a damn thing he could do about it until after the election. His mouth flattening to a thin line, he reached for the pad and pencil on the nightstand next to the bed. "Where is it? Did she give you the address?"

"Yes."

"But she told you not to give it to me," he guessed shrewdly when the other man made no move to volunteer the information. "Right?"

"Yeah," Gary muttered. "She said you would know why, though I'll be damned if I do. But I still can't tell you where she is. I promised."

He sounded so miserable, Morgan couldn't help but smile. "Don't worry about it, Gary. I've got other ways of finding her. Thanks for your help."

Hanging up, he reached for his wallet and Chase Robertson's business card. Once before, the private investigator had tracked down where she was living for him; it shouldn't be hard for him to do so again. All he had to do was follow her home from the shelter one night.

As the days leading up to the election slowly dragged, Philly would have given just about anything to have been able to cut Morgan out of her life as easily as she'd cut herself out of his. But there were constant reminders of him everywhere—billboards, posters, television and radio commercials—that always seemed to catch her when she was feeling her most vulnerable. Like it or not, she was aware of every move he made. And when he refused to let King draw him into a mudslinging campaign and instead forced the other man into a televised debate, she, like most of the voters of Maryland, sat glued to her set. Fascinated, she watched Morgan skillfully expose King's greatest weakness—when the personal attacks and all the rhetoric about rich versus poor were stripped away, he had precious little to offer the voters.

Even so, by the time election day dawned, there was still a possibility that King could pull out an upset. Holed up in her cracker box of an apartment that night, Philly perched on the edge of a sagging, overstuffed monstrosity of a chair she had picked up for practically nothing at a junk shop and anxiously watched the election returns on TV. When the Morgan-King race had been mentioned, the political analysts had refused to predict an eventual winner. Only the early, smaller districts had reported in, and at this point, it was just too close to call.

Gnawing her bottom lip, she tried to convince herself that the voters were too smart to be taken in by a man like King. Anyone with eyes and ears could see that he'd say anything, do anything, just to get elected. Morgan, on the other hand, had stood up for his principles even when he knew he was playing right into his opponent's hands. His beliefs didn't change with the rise and fall of the polls. Couldn't the voters see that?

"And now we have new tallies on one of the country's more interesting congressional races," the network anchor droned on. "Morgan Stewart II, grandson of the late Speaker of the House . . ."

Philly stiffened, her eyes trained unblinkingly on the screen while dread spilled into her stomach. Oh, God, she prayed, don't let him lose!

" . . . has had a tough race with his opponent, Hollis King, a virtual unknown six months ago who quickly got the voters' attention by trying to make Stewart's family wealth one of the issues of the campaign," the anchor continued. "The strategy apparently didn't work as well as King had hoped, however. Stewart currently leads fifty-two to forty-three percent, with fifteen percent of the votes already in, and is the projected winner. Jerry Cochran is standing by at the Stewart campaign headquarters for his victory speech, but so far there's been no sign of the Congressman. In the meantime, we'll go to the Baltimore Hilton, where King is waiting to concede defeat."

Stunned, Philly watched the man who had been a constant threat to Morgan for months now grudgingly congratulate him on his win. Relief flooded her, bringing with it a rush of tears she made no attempt to hide since there was no one there to see. It was over. Finally.

Lost in a bittersweet tide of thankfulness, she didn't hear the knock at the door until it was repeated, this time rather forcefully. Surprised, she glanced at her watch and frowned. It was almost ten o'clock, not the best time to go calling in a neighborhood that wasn't the safest in the world but the only one she could afford. Who would be visiting her, anyway? She didn't know any of her neighbors except for a nodding acquaintance, and Gary was working at the shelter.

Approaching the front door cautiously, she lifted her hand to the dead bolt but didn't unlock it. "Yes? Who's there?"

"Morgan."

She paled as her heart seemed to drop to her toes. How had he found her? And what was he doing here?

Her eyes flew in horror back to the TV. The press and his supporters were waiting for him to put in an appearance at his campaign headquarters and give his victory speech!

Hastily wiping her tear-streaked cheeks, she drew the dead bolt back and jerked open the door, intending to make it clear to him once and for all that she wanted nothing to do with him. But the words died on her tongue at the sight of him. At first glance all she saw was the navy suit he wore with ease, the appropriate red and white striped tie that he'd probably pulled askew while he waited for the returns, the flush of victory climbing his finely sculptured face. A second, closer look that she couldn't deny herself, though, revealed dark shadows of tiredness under defiant eyes and a haggardness to him that wrenched at her heart.

She wanted to reach for him then, to tell him that she knew the last two weeks had been just as hard on him as they had on her. But all she could do was stand there, knowing she had to find a way to send him away, and choke, "How did you find me?"

"I've known where you were from the day you moved into this place," he retorted. Surprising her, he strode past her into the apartment, pulled the door from her white-knuckled grasp and firmly shut it. "And no, Gary didn't tell me where you were. I hired a private investigator."

"You what?"

He nodded, not the least perturbed by her shocked confusion, and took a step toward her, cutting the space between them in half. "Damn right," he growled softly, skimming his finger over the color that stole into her cheek. "Did you think I could just let you disappear? *I love you!* There was no way on God's green earth that I was going to just let you walk away. You had to know that."

His touch was so light it was little more than a whisper, but with every word his grip on her heart tightened. "You should have let me go," she said in growing desperation. "You *have* to let me go! Can't you see that we don't belong together? We never have and we never will. Go back to your campaign head-quarters for your victory party. Go back to your life! This is my world and you don't belong here."

He looked around the nearly bare apartment that was even worse than the investigator had warned him it was. When his gaze came back to hers, it was challenging. "Why?"

Her short, humorless laugh was thick with pain. "Why? Look around you! Surely you can see this isn't the most upscale neighborhood in town. Your BMW just doesn't fit in."

"But you're here," he said quietly. "Nothing else matters."

Her heart in her throat, her eyes tortured, she shook her head in denial, dislodging his fingers from her cheek. "Don't say that," she whispered. "You'll make me believe anything's possible, and I know that it's not."

Beneath his mustache, a tender half smile curled at one corner of his mouth. "I can't believe I'm hearing this from the same woman who took on me, the gov-ernment and anyone else who dared to get in her way when she was fighting for strangers off the street," he chided, settling his hands on her shoulders. "Come on, honey, where's your optimism? If you believe you can fight and make anything possible for the homeless, why can't you believe the same thing for yourself? For us?"

She could feel herself weakening, her resolves slipping, and reached out to latch on to his wrists. *Don't listen,* a voice cautioned in her head, but deep in her heart, hoped stirred. "It's not the same," she argued even as she clung to him. "If it didn't work, we'd both be so hurt—"

"And you're not hurting now? You haven't hurt the last two weeks?"

He watched the tears spill over her lashes and slide down her cheeks and abruptly gave in to the need that had been burning in him since he'd had to leave her that last morning at the beach house. Pulling her into his arms, he wrapped her close and just held her. "Damn it, sweetheart, don't you understand?" he murmured into her hair. "It doesn't matter where we came from or how much money either one of us has or even what our jobs are. We love each other and we want the same things out of life."

"How can you say that?" she asked against his neck, crowding closer even when she knew she should be drawing away. "All I want to do is help people. You want to be Speaker of the House. That's not the same thing at all."

Beneath her negative words, he heard the hope, the need to be convinced, and grinned. Framing her face in his hands, he tilted her head back so he could look her straight in the eye. "It isn't the title I'm after," he said quietly. "It's the position itself and the power that goes with it. My grandfather helped a lot of people as Speaker and died knowing he made a difference. I want to do the same thing. With you at my side. Will you marry me?"

He said it almost defiantly, as if he half expected her to find another reason to turn him down even though he'd just laid his heart and dreams out on the line before her. Gazing up at him, her heart swelled with love. How had she ever thought she could walk away from him?

"I can't give up my work at the shelter," she warned huskily.

"Is that a yes?"

"And you can't expect me to give up fighting the injustices of the system if it means innocent people are thrown out in the streets. I've made the front page before. I probably will again."

"We'll keep a scrapbook," he tossed back, sliding his hands from her face to her upper arms to draw her up on her toes. "If there's any injustice to be fought, I plan to be right there by your side." Lowering his head until his mouth was only inches away from hers, his glittering eyes narrowed on hers. "Is that a yes?"

"You know I've never been crazy about politics—"

"Philly, I'm warning you—"

"But I'm crazy about you, Congressman," she continued softly, closing the distance between them by simply raising her chin and looping her arms around his neck. "And yes, that's a yes. I hope you know what you're setting yourself up for."

"Madness," he groaned against her mouth as he swept her up into his arms to carry her off to bed. "Sheer unadulterated madness for the next fifty years or more. I can't wait!"

Lost in the devouring hunger of his kiss, Philly was already pulling at his tie when she remembered the election. "We have to stop," she gasped, struggling to hang on to reason. "You've got a victory party to go to. Everyone's waiting for you."

"Later," he promised, pulling her down with him onto the sheets. "There'll be time for all of that later. Right now, the only victory that matters is ours."

With another wild, ravenous kiss, he drove the rest of the world right out of her head, and she didn't offer up a single word of complaint. He was right. As long as they had each other, nothing else mattered.

*   *   *   *   *

From the popular author of the bestselling title
DUNCAN'S BRIDE (Intimate Moments #349)
comes the

LINDA HOWARD

COLLECTION

Two exquisite collector's editions that contain four of
Linda Howard's early passionate love stories. To add
these special volumes to your own library, be sure
to look for:

VOLUME ONE: *Midnight Rainbow*
Diamond Bay
(Available in March)

VOLUME TWO: *Heartbreaker*
White Lies
(Available in April)

 *Silhouette Books*®

SLH92

SILHOUETTE® Desire™

The Case of the Mesmerizing Boss
DIANA PALMER

Diana Palmer's exciting new series,
MOST WANTED, begins in March with
THE CASE OF THE MESMERIZING BOSS....

Dane Lassiter—one-time Texas Ranger
extraordinaire—now heads his own group of
crack private detectives. Soul-scarred by
women, this heart-stopping private eyeful
exists only for his work—until the night his
secretary, Tess Meriwether, becomes the target
of drug dealers. Dane wants to keep her safe.
But their stormy past makes him the one man
Tess *doesn't* want protecting her....

Don't miss THE CASE OF THE MESMERIZING
BOSS by Diana Palmer, first in a lineup of
heroes MOST WANTED! In June, watch for THE
CASE OF THE CONFIRMED BACHELOR...only
from Silhouette Desire!

SDDP-1

MOST WANTED

Silhouette Special Edition

salutes

WOMEN'S OF GLORY

from Lindsay McKenna

In a country torn with conflict, in a time of bitter passions, these brave men and women wage a war against all odds...and a timeless battle for honor, for fleeting moments of glory, for the promise of enduring love.

February: RIDE THE TIGER (#721) Survivor Dany Villard is wise to the love-'em-and-leave-'em ways of war, but wounded hero Gib Ramsey swears she's captured his heart...forever.

March: ONE MAN'S WAR (#727) The war raging inside brash and bold Captain Pete Mallory threatens to destroy him, until Tess Ramsey's tender love guides him toward peace.

April: OFF LIMITS (#733) Soft-spoken Marine Jim McKenzie saved Alexandra Vance's life in Vietnam; now he needs her love to save his honor....

NORA ROBERTS

Love has a language all its own, and for centuries, flowers have symbolized love's finest expression. Discover the language of flowers—and love—in this romantic collection of 48 favorite books by bestselling author Nora Roberts.

Starting in February, two titles will be available each month at your favorite retail outlet.

In March, look for:

Irish Rose, **Volume #3**
Storm Warning, **Volume #4**

In April, look for:

First Impressions, **Volume #5**
Reflections, **Volume #6**

Collect all 48 titles and become fluent in

THE LANGUAGE of LOVE